B

She wanted him

Fenella's forefinger hesitated on the smooth white petal, then her hand fell to her side. She stared sightlessly down at the delicate flowers.

There. She had admitted it, the secret hidden under the anger and the hatred and the scorn. She wanted Dominic Maxwell.

But she was not going to succumb to a passion that had all the elements of one of nature's nastier jokes. When she made love, it would be with a man who valued her, who was prepared to give her tenderness and affection as well as sex. Making love with Dominic might have all the awesome force of a tropical storm, but like a cyclone it would only leave her broken and battered. His passion would be fundamentally destructive.

ROBYN DONALD lives in northern New Zealand with her husband and children. They love the outdoors and particularly enjoy sailing and stargazing on warm nights. Robyn doesn't remember being taught to read, but rates reading as one of her greatest pleasures, if not a vice. She finds writing intensely rewarding and is continually surprised by the way her characters develop independent lives of their own.

Books by Robyn Donald

HARLEQUIN PRESENTS
1303—NO GUARANTEES
1343—A MATTER OF WILL
1376—THE DARKER SIDE OF PARADISE
1408—A SUMMER STORM
1434—NO PLACE TOO FAR
1464—SOME KIND OF MADNESS

HARLEQUIN ROMANCE
2391—BAY OF STARS
2437—ICEBERG

Don't miss any of our special offers. Write to us at the following address for information on our newest releases.

Harlequin Reader Service
P.O. Box 1397, Buffalo, NY 14240
Canadian address: P.O. Box 603,
Fort Erie, Ont. L2A 5X3

ROBYN DONALD

Storm Over Paradise

Harlequin Books

TORONTO • NEW YORK • LONDON
AMSTERDAM • PARIS • SYDNEY • HAMBURG
STOCKHOLM • ATHENS • TOKYO • MILAN
MADRID • WARSAW • BUDAPEST • AUCKLAND

Harlequin Presents first edition November 1992
ISBN 0-373-11505-9

Original hardcover edition published in 1991
by Mills & Boon Limited

STORM OVER PARADISE

Printed in U.S.A.

CHAPTER ONE

FENELLA GARDNER frowned as she listened to her half-brother's endearingly erratic voice on the answerphone. Separating out a strand of thick straight black hair, she wound it round and round her slender forefinger as the dark brows in her olive face drew together even further.

'Anyway, I thought I'd better ring you and see what you make of it. I don't want to see him, even if he is my grandfather. He's never acknowledged my existence before; why should he start now? Ring the school as soon as you can, Fenny.'

Thinking furiously, she twirled the lock of hair until the voice of her friend and business partner, Anne Tubman, impinged. '...so I said we'd have the thing finished and framed by next Wednesday as she's leaving for England on Thursday. Sorry, Fen, I know it's pushing things, but she's prepared to pay well. Think you can do it?'

Muttering, Fenella rewound the tape and listened again, more carefully this time. Anne had promised some woman a picture of the house she'd been born in, done in Fenella's meticulous style with pen and ink and water-colours, to be ready in fewer than five days, two of which were the weekend! Oh, well, it wouldn't be the first time she had worked through. Normally it took her only a day to actually do the drawing, but she had several other orders to finish and frame in that time.

Casting a glance out of the window at the brilliant Auckland sky, tender and radiant with the promise of a New Zealand summer only a month away, she sighed, then said aloud in a resigned tone, 'At least it's fine, but the timing's going to be tight. I hope to heaven it's not

5

some old Victorian mansion decorated with wooden lace and fenced in by ornate veranda balustradings!'

But before she could ring Anne and complain to her for letting her soft heart get in the way of what was possible and what was not, Fenella rang through to the boarding school where her fourteen-year-old brother spent each term.

Fortunately Mark was able to come to the telephone. 'Where were you?' he demanded somewhat aggrievedly.

'Sketching.' Dismissing her means of livelihood with this one word, she demanded, 'Tell me exactly what the letter from James Maxwell said.'

'It was addressed to the Head, so I don't know exactly what it said, but the guts—gist of it was that I should present myself at the airport on the seventeenth of November with a current passport, and that I'd be taken to Fala'isi to stay with my grandfather for the Christmas holidays.' His voice soared, but he retained enough control to say bluntly, 'It sounded like a general barking out a command.'

'Your grandfather is not noted for his tact or lovingkindness,' Fenella retorted, her voice crisp and hard. 'What do you want to do?'

His momentary hesitation told her the answer even before he confessed awkwardly, 'Well, I suppose I want to go. At first I was furious—I'm like you, I don't like being ordered around—but I've cooled down a bit and— well, I've always been curious to know what that side of the family are like.'

Fenella too knew what it was like to wonder about your heritage. Her own father's family was completely unknown to her. 'Then of course you must go,' she said, carefully keeping the disappointment from her voice. She had been looking forward to spending Christmas with him.

'Yeah, well, only if you go too,' he said gruffly.

Shock held her silent for a moment, until she said quickly, 'That's very sweet of you, Mark, but I'm not related to the Maxwells. I wouldn't be welcome.'

'If you don't go I'm not going,' he said with the determined note in his voice which meant he wasn't going to budge.

'But Mark, you can't just say that your half sister is coming with you!' she protested, navy blue eyes turbulent with emotions she fought to control. 'I have no claim on your grandfather's hospitality.'

'You're more than just a sister to me, and have been for the past seven years. I'm not going to leave you alone for Christmas. Don't worry about it, Fenny. If he really wants to get to know me there'll be other times. I'll come home to the flat and we'll have a family Christmas as we always do.'

'Mark——'

'Fenella,' he returned, mocking her patient tone with such deadly accuracy that she laughed and yielded, although dismay still lingered in her expression.

'All right, then, but only if you're sure.' Then, because he should understand this, she added, 'But you might well be hurting your future prospects, love. Your grandfather has no time for me, and he hasn't much of a reputation for patience either. If you don't jump when he shouts he may well wash his hands of you entirely.'

'In that case I'd be well rid of him, wouldn't I?' Mark said unanswerably. 'Yes, I know he provides the money for my schooling, and yes, I know he's filthy rich, but quite frankly he sounds like a poisonous old toad to me. It's not my fault that my father and mother weren't legally married! If he dumps me, then good riddance to him, I say. I can make my own way in the world, just as you have.'

Of course he could, she thought proudly as she hung up. Mark had everything it took for success—a keen brain, determination, but, more important than all that, he had a genuinely kind heart.

Not in the least like his half-brother.

As she made her solitary dinner she couldn't banish the memories of that brother: Dominic Maxwell, her stepfather's other son. The only *legitimate* son, as he had informed them when he came to tell her mother that the man she had been married to for eight years had another wife in Australia.

Fenella's teeth worried her top lip. For all that it had been seven years ago, she remembered his visit only too well, every searing second of it.

He looked like a gladiator, she had thought at first sighting, her romantic little sixteen-year-old heart rocking oddly in her chest. With charcoal-brown hair and dark skin, several inches above six feet, and *big*, the sort of man who physically dominated a room, Dominic Maxwell had wide shoulders, long legs, big hands with long strong fingers. A truly formidable figure of a man, possessed of the brutal beauty of a warrior.

Yet for all his size he walked with the smooth rippling gait of a predator. Beneath the sophistication of his business suit his body was lean and hard with muscle, the strong thighs flexing slightly as he came in through the door of the neat suburban bungalow that had been Fenella's home during the holidays ever since the man she called Father had married her mother.

Simon Maxwell had been away on one of the extended trips he made around the Pacific Basin three or four times a year for his firm.

Only it turned out that he had been lying about the purpose of those trips. Each time Simon left them he had gone back to Australia to rejoin the family he had there, the son and father who lived in a big mansion in one of Sydney's exclusive marine suburbs, and the ailing, older wife.

Dominic Maxwell was that son, the only child of his first marriage.

The *legal* marriage, he had pointed out in his deep, cold, beautiful voice, with no thought of sparing either woman. In fact, after one oddly piercing survey he had not looked at Fenella again, keeping those icily green eyes fixed on her mother's shuttered face.

Simon Maxwell was a bigamist; for eight years he had lived a double life, juggling his responsibilities with such skill that they had only just caught up with them.

In case his bigamous wife disbelieved him, Dominic had incontrovertible proof. Fenella thought she might have forgiven him the harsh relish he seemed to take in confronting them with details of her stepfather's perfidy if he hadn't been so coldly, scornfully disgusted by the sordidness of the whole business. She could still see the curl of his hard, sculptured mouth as her mother began to weep.

'I'm sorry, madam,' he said icily, 'but you must have realised that this was likely to happen. He won't be coming back—my grandfather has made it a condition of his forgiveness that he never see you again. And Simon is not going to give up the prospect of a fortune for the pleasures of this love-nest.' Ignoring her mother's sobs, he had continued, 'However, as we accept that your son has some claim on him, my grandfather is prepared to pay for his keep and schooling. No more. You've already collected a considerable sum of money from the Maxwells, money you had no right to as it belonged to my mother.' He looked contemptuously down at her mother's bent head. 'My father, as perhaps you didn't realise, has no money. There will be no large settlements this time, madam.'

Made furious by both his tone of voice and the cruel words he was saying, Fenella had looked across at her mother, expecting her to throw such an insulting suggestion back at his throat, but to her shame and chagrin her mother had, after one horrified look, merely continued weeping, her softly ravishing beauty unmarred by the poignant, piteous tears.

Fenella had never forgotten the disdain in Dominic Maxwell's expression, the subtle darkening of the fascinating pale green eyes, the way the gladiator's face had hardened into a mask of scorn.

He had gone then, but three months later, after her mother had swallowed the sleeping pills she had saved so carefully, he returned, and this time he looked at her with the same contempt.

Stony-faced, Fenella had stared back, hating him, hating everything that he stood for, holding her small bewildered brother's hand in her slender one. Her mother's suicide note was engraved in letters of fire on her brain.

> I can't go on. Please forgive me, and, Fenny, look after Mark.

'He'll have to go to boarding school,' Dominic said impatiently.

Mark's lip trembled as his hot little paw clutched Fenella's tightly. She, who had spent her life since that bigamous second marriage packed away at a very good girls' boarding school, said fiercely, 'He's too little. I'll leave school and look after him.'

His brows had climbed as he looked her over. 'How old are you?'

'Sixteen, but I——'

'The last thing you'll want is a small boy interfering with your life.'

She bit her lip, stopping when she saw the shimmering ice of his gaze rest thoughtfully on the betraying little movement. As if she hadn't spoken he went on in that hard, detached voice, 'And seven is not too young to go away from home. That's how old I was when I went to prep school. I'll organise it.'

'Mark,' Fenella had commanded in her gentlest tone, 'run into the kitchen and get yourself a drink and a biscuit.' She waited until he was gone before continuing belligerently, 'It's not Mark's fault that your father married my mother without divorcing your mother first. You have no need to punish him by packing him off to school. You may have enjoyed prep school, but I hated it when I was sent away. Mark's only a little boy, he's been used to a loving home life. My mother adored him, she——'

'She adored him so much that she committed suicide rather than see him grow up,' he said with such casual cruelty that she could only stare at him while sudden shaming tears filled her eyes.

Gulping, she searched for a handkerchief, but she had used hers to mop up a sudden burst of tears from Mark, so she was forced to sniff while she dashed the tears from her eyes with the back of her hand. The white linen one thrust into her hand was reluctantly accepted.

Waiting until she had blown her nose, Dominic Maxwell said with slightly less antagonism, 'Hiding behind a cloak of sentimental drivel isn't going to help either you or Mark. Your mother chose to leave you and the boy in an impossible situation. You can't look after him; even if you knew how to, the social welfare here would never allow it. I've checked with them, and they say they're prepared to accept our plans for him. Boarding school is the only way out. It will probably do him the world of good if he's been spoiled and indulged by his mother.'

She lifted her head proudly. 'I hate you,' she said quietly, angry colour suffusing the clear golden olive of her skin.

The wide shoulders moved in a shrug. Completely unperturbed, he said calmly, 'I'm not going to lose any sleep over the unbridled emotions of an undisciplined adolescent.'

Even now, seven years later, Fenella still cringed with humiliation at the thought of what she had done then. Smarting at the mocking amusement in his smile, her emotions shredded raw by the twin tragedies of her stepfather's betrayal and her mother's death, baffled and foiled in her hopes for the future, she lost her precarious control and lashed out at the man she blamed for everything that had happened.

For such a big man he moved fast, but surprise gave her the edge and he couldn't quite deflect the open-handed slap she aimed at his face, connecting across his cheek. It felt like smashing against a rock. With a smothered gasp she wrenched her painful hand away. Horrified, she watched while the swarthy skin paled, then filled with dark colour. Then her gaze crawled across the stark features to connect with his. Such molten fury seethed there that she took an involuntary step backwards.

But his hand came out with the speed of a striking snake, imprisoning her wrist in a grip that numbed her whole arm. 'You little bitch,' he said, the silky words freezing the blood in her veins.

She didn't know what punishment she expected. Certainly not the sudden downward swoop of his head, and the fierce kiss looted from her soft young mouth.

In a way it had been the end of innocence, that kiss. Oh, it wasn't the first; she had been kissed several times before, but they had been the tentative, shy embraces of boys not much older than she was, and although she had liked them she had not been much impressed, even wondering what all the song and dance was about.

But this was far from tentative; Dominic kissed her with the heated skill of experience, bringing her body into close contact with his, forcing her startled lips open so that he could plunder the soft depths of her mouth.

Fenella should have been repelled by the deep intimacy of the kiss, but somehow her virginal shrinking became transmuted into a more instinctive response, and she sighed, allowing him complete access, lashes drooping to hide her wide glazed eyes, reacting with an innocent, unshackled abandon.

The scope of her senses narrowed, sharpened, so that she was conscious only of his taste, dark and mysteriously male, and the heat that sizzled along her nerves as his tongue thrust in a movement that made her stiffen in hungry need. Fire clutched at her body, fountained up from deep inside her to melt the area between her legs, across her breasts, touching every cell and nerve with its honeyed flame. For the first time in her life she felt passion.

Her heart speeded up, blocking out all other sounds, and she breathed in his scent, masculine, incredibly potent to her untutored senses.

He overpowered her, his arms binding her strongly to the taut threat of his big lean body. A muffled sound forced itself up from deep in his throat and one hand moved down her back, pushing her hard against him so that her hips met his in a single thrust of such power and sensual promise that she was drenched in a shower of languorous enticement.

His voice was deep and husky as he bit gently down the length of her throat, although she couldn't discern the harsh impeded words. Against her skin she felt the fine trembling of his hands, the heavy thud of a heartbeat that drowned out hers. Excitement, pure and sharp as a crystal, pierced her, mingling with the hot laziness of desire. She whimpered, afire with pleasure yet wanting so much more, at the mercy of overwhelming primeval instincts.

Somehow he must have managed to unfasten her demure shirt, because when she felt his slightly rough hand against her breast she gasped at the exquisite spasm of sensation that seared up her spine as his thumb found the sensitive aureole. And, although she knew she should not be letting him do this, she couldn't overcome the dazed wantonness that blocked all her thought processes, subverting the calm common sense she had always rather prided herself on.

His mouth on the soft skin of her breast was heated and searching, almost cruel, but she welcomed his desperation, reading in it an eagerness as great as hers.

A faint sound at the back of her throat died as he found the soft core and suckled strongly, drawing the suddenly rigid little nipple into his mouth. Fenella began to tremble, rigours loosening her knees. She had to clutch him to stay upright, her pulse hammering so hard that she thought she might faint.

Her whole being went up in a conflagration. Mindless, rapturous, she sank into sensation, aware of nothing but the experienced savagery of his mouth and the violent pleasure it was giving her.

And then he lifted his head, searched her dazzled face with eyes darkened to stormy jade, and almost flung her across the room. Gasping, her mouth a crushed rose, she stared at him with frustrated bewilderment, every cell in her body aching with frustration and desire as she dragged the shirt back across her bare breasts, feeling now the first slimy tendrils of humiliation.

'It seems you're just as ready to buy security with your body as your mother was,' he said savagely. 'Sorry, I'm not so easily seduced as my father.'

White-faced, thoughts tumbling around in her head in a dizzy cacophony, Fenella pushed a hand through the blue-black cascade of her hair, trying to find some point of reference in all of this, some sort of sanity in the whirlwind of emotions that had blown up so suddenly.

'Dominic——' she whispered, holding out an imploring hand, hoping for some sort of comfort in this new realm of the senses to which she had been so ruthlessly introduced.

'Mr Maxwell to you,' he said brutally. 'It's no use, Fenella, I'm not going to let a juvenile slut work her wiles on me. Do as you're bid and I'll see to it that the boy gets into a decent school. Try anything else and I'll throw you both into the gutter where you belong. But rest assured of one thing—I'm going to make sure that neither of you ever gets another cent from Maxwells to waste!'

Numbly she watched him stride out of the room like a gladiator on the way to the arena, cruel, merciless, a man to fear and respect, a man brutalised by his capacity to inflict pain.

Now, shivering in the late afternoon sun, Fenella was glad that she had never seen him again. Seven years had passed, but the thought of him still had the power to make her feel sick with shame.

What would he be like now? Even tougher, she decided with a small grimace. His father had died three years ago without ever attempting to get in touch with Mark, and his grandfather had retired, so Dominic Maxwell was now in charge of the enormous construction company that had ridden triumphantly through the perils of that most perilous of fields and had diversified to become one of the most important conglomerates in the world.

Such power at the age of thirty; she hoped he wielded it a little less brutally that he had with her.

His name turned up quite frequently in newspapers and magazines; Fenella hated herself for reading the articles, but something impelled her on. She knew that he was extremely good at his job, ruthless and tough when such traits were needed, strangely compassionate at other times. She knew that, although he had been seen about with women, always beautiful, usually rich, there had never been anyone the columnists thought him likely to marry until recently, when one Sarah Springfellow had appeared on the scene.

Daughter of an old, very rich family, one that figured largely in Australian history, Miss Springfellow had been tipped as the future Mrs Dominic Maxwell. Fenella thought she looked pretty and sweet, although nowhere near tough enough to cope with him.

But then it would probably be one of those marriages that were more like mergers, she decided, pitying the woman.

It would take a woman of unusual qualities to make any sort of satisfying life with a hard, ambitious man who had a calculator for a heart and a computer for a brain. And if Fenella ever recalled the immense sexual charisma that had knocked her so completely sideways seven years ago, she had managed to bury the memories so deep that she was convinced she had merely overreacted, as any innocent adolescent would, to the first sexually knowledgeable man to make love to her.

Mark rang again the next day. 'I told them I wouldn't come without you,' he said without preamble.

'What—*oh*! Who? Who did you tell?'

'My grandfather, I suppose. Ultimately.' It was not difficult to detect some nervousness in his muffled laugh. 'Some secretary person rang, a man called Philip Someone-or-other. He started to tell me what to do, so I just said I wasn't coming unless you came with me, and after a while he seemed to get the message. He said very sniffily that he'd have to let Mr Maxwell know. End of phone call.' He mimicked a fussy male voice. '"But Mr Maxwell does not like having his plans obstructed. We have ascertained when your examinations finish and Mr Maxwell wants you to arrive at Fala'isi on the seventeenth of November inst." Or it might have been "ult",' he finished cheerfully.

Fenella drew in a sharp breath, then expelled it in a shaky chuckle. 'Well, if you're prepared to miss the chance of meeting your grandfather and enjoying a holiday in the South Seas, I suppose I should be prepared to endure the same if he agrees. But he probably won't, Mark, so don't be disappointed, will you?'

'Nope. You could do with a holiday, anyway, apart from anything else. You've been working too darned hard for the last four years, ever since you decided to start up with Anne. She had a fortnight off last year, so it's time you had a rest too.'

'Staying with your grandfather isn't likely to be much of one,' she pointed out drily.

There was an arrested silence, then Mark asked anxiously, 'Would you rather not come, Fenny?'

She could have kicked herself for not considering this reaction, and moved hastily to reassure him. 'Darling, I'm going to enjoy it very much. I believe Fala'isi is absolutely beautiful; don't they call it the nearest place to Paradise? If we go, I'll enjoy it, don't worry.'

Even if it kills me, she thought, her stomach feeling oddly hollow. But of course they'll say no.

'That's the way,' said Mark, restored to his usual cheerfulness. 'Hey, if Dominic is my half-brother and you're my half-sister, what relation are you to each other?'

'None. For which both of us give much thanks.' The light flippancy of her tone was rewarded with a chuckle, before he launched into a description of his latest titanic battle on the squash court.

She had just hung up when the telephone rang again. Mark had this habit of remembering something of vital importance as soon as he hung up and ringing back, so she picked up the receiver and laughed into it, 'What now, darling?'

There was enough of a silence on the other end to tell her that it was not Mark. Mouth quirking wryly, she prepared to amend matters when a voice she had never forgotten, deep and smooth as velvet, so at variance with what she knew of his character, demanded curtly, 'Fenella? Fenella Gardner?'

Her mouth dried completely but she managed to croak, 'Yes.' And pride compelled her to ask, 'Who's speaking?'

'Dominic Maxwell.'

Fenella inhaled sharply, fighting for control. After a moment she managed to murmur in a voice sugary with malice, 'Ah, Mr Maxwell, what can I do for you?'

'You can tell your brother that you're not coming with him to Fala'isi,' he said with insulting brusqueness.

Challenge sparkled in the narrowed blue depths of her eyes. 'I've already told him that,' she returned dulcetly. 'Unfortunately he wants me to go. And he's extraordinarily stubborn.'

'I don't think you'd enjoy it.' The words were delivered in a bored voice, but she recognised the threat.

Fenella's heart jolted; she had to remind herself that it was seven years since she had seen him, and she had grown up a lot in those seven years.

'No,' she said, implying a yawn, 'I doubt very much whether I will.'

'But you're still determined to come.'

She retorted limpidly, 'Mark is determined that I should.'

'I see.' He paused before finishing with insolent casualness, 'Very well, then. Of course you'll have to pay your own way.'

'Naturally,' she said with more than a hint of hauteur, baring her teeth at the receiver. 'Goodbye, Mr Maxwell.'

And hung up, feeling obscurely as though somehow, after all these years, she had levelled a little of the crushing load of humiliation she still carried whenever she thought of Dominic Maxwell.

A week later she was sitting in the economy class section of an airliner, headed for Fala'isi. Beside her a large woman read a magazine with the determination of someone who feels it necessary to keep her mind busy. Somewhere up in the first class section of the plane was Mark.

Fenella couldn't prevent the appreciative smile that widened her soft mouth. The slight had been conceived with real flair, she decided, flair in which she detected the fine Italian hand of Dominic Maxwell. To have her ensconced with the *hoi-polloi* in economy, while Mark lounged in the luxury paid for with Maxwell money in first, was cleverly insulting.

Of course, with their opinion of her they couldn't be expected to know that she would have had immense pleasure in turning down the offer of any monetary help.

But her amusement didn't last long. Not for the first time, she wondered why his grandfather wanted to see Mark. It wouldn't be for any normal reason, she knew, like wanting to get to know his grandson. If James Maxwell had a sentimental bone in his body it was so well hidden that a post-mortem probably wouldn't turn it up.

Always providing the old devil ever died and wasn't just carried off in a clap of thunder with a strong whiff of sulphur.

Since the traumatic events of seven years ago Fenella's perusal of various magazines and newspapers had broadened her knowledge of the background to the Maxwell power. James had come from poverty to build his empire with hard work, judicious ruthlessness, and an uncanny flair for sniffing out the trends and applying them to the marketplace. They were a reclusive family who rarely appeared in the social pages, but they were highly thought of in Government and business circles in Australia and throughout the Pacific. Simon Maxwell had been James's only child, and according to the newspapers it was Dominic who was now fully in charge.

She had read of Simon's death in one of those magazines, learning that he had taken very little part in the family firm, and that the wife who had been an invalid for most of her life was still alive.

Fenella closed her eyes for a moment, recalling the complexity of emotions that had surged through her when she read of his death. Anger came first; he had brought them all such pain. But then, if he hadn't persuaded her mother into that bigamous marriage, Mark wouldn't have been born. Although she remembered that he had been angry about Mark's arrival; the only time she had heard them arguing, Simon had told her mother that he had not wanted children.

Still, presented with a *fait accompli*, he had been an amiable father, from what she had seen when she came home from boarding school. And to her he had always been distant but pleasant.

Now, staring out at the billowy white top of the cloud layer, so firm-looking yet so insubstantial, she remembered that when she had gone to tell Mark of his father's death it was to find that he already knew. A Maxwell minion had rung the headmaster at the expensive school that Maxwell influence had got Mark into, and Maxwell money paid for, and the headmaster had carefully and compassionately told him.

Fenella had looked at her twelve-year-old brother, tall and slim but already showing promise of the build that marked his half-brother, and her heart had ached for him. As ever, he had reassured her.

'I don't really remember him,' he said honestly. 'He was away so much... Anyway, I've got you, Fenny.'

'Yes, you've got me,' she said, risking a hug.

He had returned it with interest, and she had been surprised to realise that she was sorry for Simon Maxwell, who had died unloved and unmissed by his younger son, despised by his older. Not much of an epitaph, she thought grimly.

The flight to Fala'isi was smooth, the food and entertainment dispensed with pleasant efficiency, and Fenella even had a chance to see the first class, because Mark came back and insisted, charming the stewardess with such ease that Fenella realised with a jolt that he had inherited his father's genial sophistication. It was fortunate he had also an integrity that certainly hadn't come from Simon.

She had been back in her own seat for an hour or so when at last the island appeared on the horizon like something out of a dream, a jewelled piece of paradise set in the limitless Pacific. A dramatic interior of volcanic peaks, some brilliantly green, some stark pinnacles of bare rock, was surrounded by a narrow coastal plain patchworked into plantations, dotted by tiny villages. A reef looped the island, its thin white necklace separating the intense lapis lazuli of the sea from the vivid sapphire and aquamarine of the lagoon.

It was breathtakingly beautiful, as magical as every travel poster of every South Sea Island, a mirage on the edge of enchantment, almost as insubstantial as the cloud castles they had flown above.

And then they were down and it was all very substantial, from the warm purple dusk to the scent of frangipani in the air, the islanders manning the Customs

desks and Agriculture and Immigration, the tearful re-
unions and the leis of brilliant, scented flowers flung
about necks everywhere.

Mark caught her up, his eyes bright with excitement.
'Hey, this is choice, isn't it? Where do we go now?'

'Through the door there.'

He bent to pick up her suitcase, so Fenella was the
first to notice the man who waited for them. Almost she
tripped, then, challenging Dominic Maxwell's inimical
gaze, her chin came up and she said to her brother, 'Over
there, love.'

'Where—oh! Yes, I remember him.' And with no great
appreciation, judging by the note in his uncertain voice.
'Rats,' he muttered. 'I wish my wretched voice would
settle down!'

'It won't take long, and it's much better than it used
to be. Anyway, I'll bet both your grandfather and
Dominic had wobbly voices when they were growing up.'

He gave a lopsided smile at this attempt at reassurance and set off through the crowd of eager passengers;
as she followed, Fenella realised that Dominic was
waiting in the entrance to a small room. So the meeting
was to be private. Thank heavens! She was already embarrassed by the interested glances and unhidden spec-
ulation of the onlookers.

But it wasn't at her that Dominic looked when at last
the door closed behind them. That ice-cold survey
scanned her brother. Mark, she was pleased to see, bore
it well and manfully, although his cheeks were touched
with colour when at last it ended.

Dominic said in his deep smooth imperturbable voice,
'Welcome to Fala'isi.'

'Thank you,' Mark returned politely.

'Is that all your gear?'

They both nodded. Dominic transferred his gaze to
Fenella, and she almost cried out loud at the flat implacable contempt she saw there. 'I've already ordered
a taxi for you,' he said.

Shock jolted her normal thinking processes into stunned acquiescence. Recovering with sluggish slowness, she said, 'Thank you.'

Beside her Mark stirred uneasily. With a swift admonitory look she said, 'I'll see you later, love.'

'Just tell the driver where to go.' A pointed second and Dominic finished, 'He's already been paid.'

She gave Mark a kiss, a pat on the shoulder, picked up her suitcase and left, so angry she was barely able to see.

Outside one of the islanders beamed at her and said, 'You can't come to Fala'isi without a lei, girl. Here,' as she tossed a thick scented rope of flowers about her neck.

Fenella thanked her. At any other time she would have been thrilled by the soft cool necklace of pink and cream frangipani, but tears of rage and frustration blinded her; she stumbled, and someone caught her, a masculine voice saying with a slight slur, 'Upsidaisy, little lady! You want to look where you're going.'

'Thank you,' she returned automatically, trying to pull away.

The hands holding her tightened. 'How about having a drink with me? You look as though you could use it.'

Her swift upwards glance revealed a pleasant-looking man in his early twenties. A faint aroma of alcohol revealed that he had perhaps had one more beer than was desirable; that, and the warm sensuality of the soft air, probably led him to be a little more forward than he would have been back in New Zealand.

'No, thanks,' she said, trying to let him down gently. Her smile had a hard, glittery quality, but she judged him harmless and was grateful for his support.

'Come on,' he coaxed, smiling down at her with an ingenuous charm that was probably very potent most of the time. 'I'm quite a nice person, really.'

'I'm sure you are,' she was saying when a hand on her arm swung her around and Mark's voice demanded curtly, 'Is this guy bothering you, Fenny?'

'No——' Her eyes travelled past his concerned face to meet those of the man behind him. She gave a little gasp, then dragged hers away and turned back to the young man, saying, 'This is my brother. Thank you for catching me.'

But he hadn't seen the lethal expression on Dominic's face. Smiling a little foolishly, he said, 'Why don't you both come—— '

'The lady is going with me.' A simple statement, delivered by Dominic in a level, emotionless tone, but the young man, looking up, read danger in both tone and face, gulped, and disappeared with more circumspection than valour.

Mark looked at his half-brother with the beginning of hero-worship, then back at Fenella's wary face. 'It's all right,' he said, his voice cracking with emotion, 'it was a misunderstanding. You're coming with us. Dominic thought you'd already booked into a hotel. You didn't tell me that you and he had spoken on the phone.'

From the faint chagrin in his words she realised that Dominic had made the best of what could possibly have been an irretrievable mistake; it was a clever move, for he had even managed to put her slightly in the wrong.

Fenella's wariness increased. It would not do to underestimate Dominic Maxwell, and it appeared that for some reason he did not want Mark to suspect his real emotions. What did the Maxwells want with her brother after ignoring him for all these years?

'I see,' she said slowly, relinquishing her suitcase to a man who had appeared at her elbow with a luggage trolley.

She looked up to meet the enigmatic coolness of Dominic's astounding green eyes, realising with a terrified thump of her heart that he knew what she was thinking and was coldly amused by it. What was going on? Her eyes narrowed, long silky lashes falling to hide their depths as she looked away, aware that she was whistling against the wind. This man had fought and won wars with huge international corporations. He was not going to be intimidated by a woman he had already written off as a slut.

And it appeared that for some nefarious reason he was going to do his best to undermine her standing with Mark. And the reason was probably that he thought her a bad influence on a growing boy!

Fenella ran a nervous hand down over the hip of her white skirt, enjoying the feel of the cotton and linen mix under her fingers. It was only in the last year that she had been able to afford to buy good clothes, and this was part of a set of mix-and-match pieces that she had splurged on. With it she wore a matching jacket over an ice-blue singlet top. It was already too hot, but she was not going to take the jacket off.

Not under Dominic Maxwell's knowing, insulting gaze.

'We're going by helicopter,' Mark was saying eagerly as they followed the man with the trolley down a short passage and out into the humid sunlight again. The helicopter was waiting, rotors already turning, engines chop-chop-chopping in the damp air.

Fenella bit her lip, and bit it again when she was inside the wretched machine and she realised that Dominic was going to pilot it. Helicopters were not her favourite mode of transport, but she wasn't going to let on so that he could be amused by her fear. At least she wasn't sitting beside him. Mark was there, looking younger and impossibly eager, just like the little boy he had been when his half-brother came to break up their home. Turning around, he grinned.

Although she nodded brightly she had the uncomfortable feeling that one person at least was not fooled. As she turned her head to look out of the side window she could feel the icy trail of Dominic's eyes down her profile. Like the stealthy hunter she compared him to, he missed nothing.

Then they were in the air, her involuntary gasp lost in the thunderous noise of the motors. After five minutes or so when the dust had cleared and the sea and sky had stopped whirling hideously in front of her eyes, she forced her eyes open.

Below her lay the island as she had seen it coming in on the airliner, only closer, much more intimately, the folded hills crumpled like textured silk above the thickly settled and planted lowlands, the silver threads of waterfalls and streams, the clouds massing mysteriously about improbably stark peaks.

They flew over the capital of the island, a small compact town where only the largest buildings were higher than a coconut palm and the houses were almost hidden in thick growth, and then on, around the dramatic central mountains rather than over them.

Fenella's interest kept her nervousness subdued. The colours fascinated her into catching her breath; the acid green of the vegetation, dotted with crimson and scarlet canopies of large spreading trees that bloomed everywhere. Flamboyants, she thought, and how appropriate the name was!

The helicopter chirred steadily on, over a bay where coconut palms flowered like pinwheels above crisply gleaming sand, over a village of thatched roofs tucked above a wide circle of stones that had to be a fish-trap in the glittering lagoon. Canoes were pulled up on the white sand; as, enchanted, she peered down, she saw the people in one out on the lagoon wave, even caught the flash of white in dark faces as they smiled.

Around the reef there were small islands, *motu*, exquisitely right for a seduction or a movie, she thought with some irony.

But the colours! Verdant greens and brilliant blues, purple where coral showed close to the surface, a gleaming enamelled lagoon with an infinite variety of shades edging into the magnificent wrinkled blue, dark as her eyes, of the open water beyond the reef's sheltering arms.

Fenella thought she could never tire of gazing at those colours; her artist's eyes gleamed and she wished achingly that she had the skill to do them justice with paint.

The helicopter swerved, tilted, and headed towards a large complex, starkly white against the verdant greenery in an area where the jungle came down to the coast. Acutely conscious of her hands clenching into fists, Fenella deliberately relaxed them, concentrating on staying calm.

The house was set by itself at the end of the road at the edge of a small bay. Over a jungle-covered headland was a village where thatched roofs provided a piquant contrast to the shiny modernity of corrugated iron ones. Still breathing deeply and slowly, she noted a large building in the centre of the village; perhaps a meeting-house? More canoes were drawn up on the glittering white sand beneath the swaying coconut palms; as they swooped low over the village children ran out and waved.

Fenella gulped, closing her eyes momentarily before forcing them open. They were dropping fast now over the thick growth of the headland; turning her head, she fixed her gaze on to a large, very luxurious cruiser anchored in a pool in the little bay out from the house. By concentrating hard she could follow the channel of deeper water that wound its way past the village and out across the dangerous coral heads of the lagoon to the gap in the reef.

She even managed to look down as they came in to a concrete pad set well back from the large sprawling house. Her eyes found a swimming pool and a series of shaded terraces, solar panels on the roof, shutters at each window, gardens laid out with charming irregularity, and then they were down, and the engines cut off as a lithe islander ran out from the shade towards them.

Fenella's breath sounded loudly inside her head. She heard Mark chuckle in the resounding silence, then Dominic Maxwell said, 'Welcome to Maxwell's Reach.'

CHAPTER TWO

'WHEW!' Mark said inelegantly, jumping down. He leaned in to give a hand to Fenella. 'It's hot!'

'This is the drier side of the island,' Dominic informed him. 'It's also more sheltered, so the tradewinds don't have a chance to cool the air.'

Mark set his sister on her feet. 'All right?'

'Yes, of course.'

She tried to make her voice as calm and composed as it normally was, but something must have given her away, for he gave her a quick hug and said bracingly, 'It's over now. You can relax.'

And while Fenella watched with an ironic little smile he bounded around to the other side of the helicopter and began to quiz his half-brother about the possibility of learning how to fly the machine.

Dominic's reply was succinct, almost curt, but Fenella saw Mark grin, and decided dismally that if the Maxwells really did want to wean Mark away from her influence, the chance of learning to pilot a helicopter would be an excellent beginning. Did they think it was time to collect on the investment they had made in Mark's education? But why?

Dominic was very definitely in charge of Maxwell Construction, and anyway, he didn't look the sort to want to give up any power at all, especially not to the son of a woman he considered little better than a slut. Besides, from her reluctant research Fenella had learned that the firm was very well served by its executives.

She wouldn't, she thought with a slight shiver, like to be an inefficient executive in any business that Dominic Maxwell controlled. Her eyes travelled warily over his lithe figure, lingering on the wide shoulders and poised, athletic body. The size of him was enough to terrify the wits out of anyone who wasn't doing their job properly, but it wasn't his size that automatically caught the eye. Ruthlessness hung like an aura about him, a cold dominance revealed in few men.

She had never forgotten it. Bruised and almost broken against the hard edge of his cruelty, she had struggled for years to convince herself that she had no need to worry about Dominic Maxwell's opinion of her.

Now she wasn't so sure about anything. Perhaps he and James Maxwell had decided that the king was not enough, that they needed to train a crown prince.

Certainly, Dominic's voice when he spoke to Mark was not anywhere near as cuttingly cold as when he spoke to her. Not that it could be called warm, either; if anything it was neutral, but the natural beauty of his tone made it pleasant to listen to. And Mark didn't seem at all upset by the man or his voice.

'Come on,' her brother said cheerfully, 'come on out of the sun, daydreamer! Here, give me your case.'

'No, Hapi will bring them in.' Dominic looked over Fenella's head and to her astonishment the swarthy sternness of his face was banished by a grin at the man who came up from the direction of the house.

Oh, lord, she thought faintly. Smiling, the man was altogether too much, his natural sexual charisma intensified into a blaze of sensuality, potent as a mind-warping drug, and, she thought dismally, probably as addictive.

Then his eyes fell on her fascinated face, and although the smile stayed the quality changed so that it was tinged with contempt. Down that unsparing gaze went, past the scooped neck of her singlet, over the lush swell of her breasts beneath the white jacket, to linger on the long line of her thighs, stripping her with overt and brutal deliberation, humiliating her with the salacious lust in his mind.

Colour rushed to her cheeks, then ebbed, leaving her pale except for her lipstick, but her eyes met his with level steadiness, refusing to show any emotion, not even defiance. Behind her she could hear Mark and Hapi getting the cases from the helicopter; beyond that nothing but the thundering roar of the waves on the barrier reef.

The hard mouth twisted. 'Welcome to Maxwell's Reach,' Dominic Maxwell repeated, not attempting to conceal the undertone of mockery to the words. He escorted her along the path beneath the coconut palms to where the house lay basking beside the warm waters of the lagoon.

It was built of coral stone, great white blocks of it, and inside it was cool and dim, with tiled floors and huge windows looking out on to arcaded courtyards where water trickled and green things grew.

The housekeeper was a grey-haired woman of what seemed to be mixed Island and European descent, tall and majestic. Her stern gaze didn't soften when she welcomed Fenella, but there was definitely a warming as she smiled at Mark. Par for the course, Fenella thought sardonically. No doubt she would soon get accustomed to being treated like a leper.

'I'll take Mark to his room,' Dominic said crisply, 'if you'll show Miss Gardner where she's to sleep, Mari.'

So they *had* prepared a room for her! Storing this away in her mind, Fenella accompanied the older woman down a wide cool arcaded corridor to a room that looked out on to the pool. A spiky plant like a New Zealand flax stood to one side, its green and gold leaves glowing in the merciless sunlight.

'If there's anything you need, miss, tell me,' Mari said, opening a door in the wall. 'Here's the bathroom, and in here, through this other door, is the dressing-room. I hope you'll be comfortable.'

'Thank you, I'm sure I shall.'

'Perhaps you would like a shower, and then there'll be lunch, in an hour, out on the terrace.'

'Thank you,' Fenella smiled, and the woman smiled back, without much warmth but at least without the elemental antagonism that iced over Dominic's eyes.

'One of the maids will be along soon to unpack for you. If you show her what you want to change into she'll see that it's pressed in time for lunch.'

Fenella said quietly, 'I'll unpack for myself, thank you, but I'd be grateful for the ironing.'

For a moment she thought the woman was going to object, but she merely inclined her head and replied regally, 'Certainly, miss.'

Left alone, Fenella stood for a moment looking about her. They might, she thought grimly, not have wanted her within a thousand miles of this millionaire's holiday bach, but they certainly hadn't given her anything like the servants' quarters.

The room was as big as her flat in Auckland, the walls plastered with what seemed to be a fine-grained stucco, while the ceiling was supported by heavy, dark beams. The tiled floor, walls and ceiling were all chalk-white; so was the bedspread on the enormous bed, with the addition of thin blue stripes woven into the fabric. Two cane chairs were upholstered in the same material and the whole was warmed by cushions in melon colours with a scattering of blues.

On one wall a painting of the island throbbed with the inconceivable fecundity of the tropics, yet hinted at a darker side to the beauty. A superb ceramic bowl, blue as the waters in the lagoon, held exquisite white moth orchids on top of a dark carved chest.

It was luxurious and brilliantly decorated, cool and welcoming, yet Fenella shivered as she stood there in the sultry air.

With a firm command to herself to stop being so fanciful, she opened her suitcase and began to unpack. Almost certainly the last person who had slept in that opulent bed had brought more clothes, but hers were of good quality and she had bought skilfully. And she most emphatically didn't give a fig what the Maxwells thought of her wardrobe! They had made their opinion of her abundantly clear, but she didn't care, her whole concern was for Mark.

Leaving the skirt and top she intended to wear on the bed, she retired to the bathroom, where she spent some minutes eyeing with awe the inordinately expensive toiletries in a cupboard. Not a package had been opened; were they provided new for each guest?

Sturdily, with a wry smile, she set out her own boxes and bottles, such as they were. Good, but not in the least exclusive; grinning at her reflection, she thought those words could well describe her. She was exceptionally lucky to have been blessed with her mother's superb skin and the kind of bones that showed it off. And if her eyes were more navy than blue, and her olive skin a little sallow—well, tension and a few late nights explained that.

At least, she thought happily, she didn't have to worry about sunburn. Unbidden, there popped into her mind an image of Dominic, the magnificent angles and planes of his face covered with skin so intense a copper that it had to be the result of a naturally dark complexion deepened by a lot of sun. Against that swarthy skin his brows and lashes were black as sin; his colouring might have been chosen to emphasise the unexpected, stunning ice green of his eyes.

Appalled, Fenella dragged her mind away; she had enough on her mind without sighing over a man's eyes, for heaven's sake, especially when the man was Dominic Maxwell!

The shower was heavenly, the pressure strong and infinitely adjustable. Fenella groaned with voluptuous pleasure as she washed off the grime of the journey and dried herself with a huge pale peach towel, before making up with a spare hand, although, as always, her lipstick was a definite and emphatic shade. Without colouring, her mouth looked almost unnaturally red, soft and unguarded. She always made sure she hid that betraying vulnerability.

Back in the bedroom her skirt and top were hanging crisply pressed on a coathanger. Brows drawn together, she surveyed the skirt, a simple cotton enlivened with flowers in turquoise, royal blue and shocking pink splashed on a white background, then shrugged. Was it too gaudy? What did one wear to lunch at a millionaire's bach beside a tropical lagoon?

Mouth straightening, she slid the skirt over her head. She would soon learn if she had miscalculated. And the skirt and sandals were cool, the white silk singlet top decent but airy, and loose enough to banish the thin bra beneath to proper obscurity.

But when she was dressed she stood for a moment in front of the huge mirror, her brows drawn together as she wound a lock of hair about her finger and surveyed herself. She had never worried about her liking for singlet tops before, but now she wondered whether perhaps she was just a little too voluptuous to wear them. There seemed to be rather a lot of golden-olive skin exposed, and when she moved the curves of her breasts appeared above the scooped neckline.

Defiantly she unwound the strand of hair and patted it back into place. She was not going to let caution drive her natural tastes underground. OK, so there was a fair amount of skin revealed, but most of it was on her shoulders and arms. Only a prude could object to that!

Voices led her to the group sitting beneath the deep overhang of the roof that formed an open-air room like a Hawaiian lanai. It was easy enough to pick out Mark's, pleasantly shy but not over-awed, and another, deeper and older. The wicked grandfather, no doubt. Nerves flickered for a moment in Fenella's stomach. Feeling foolish and cowardly, she stopped and drew a deep breath.

'If you went a little closer you could hear every word they're saying,' Dominic said from just behind her. 'But I don't think they're telling secrets.'

His sardonic voice made her whirl about, hand clenched to her heart. He was standing too close, watching her with a mocking smile. Fenella took an involuntary step backwards and his smile sharpened.

'My grandfather's not in the habit of divulging secrets to anyone, let alone a fourteen-year-old boy. Did you think you might hear something interesting?' he asked, surveying the pulse that jumped in her throat with a narrowed intent gaze.

'Of course not!' Not for anything was she going to tell him that she had stopped for a few seconds to collect her composure. Forcing her fingers to relax, she dropped her hand to her side and asked sweetly, 'Shall we join them?'

Without waiting for an answer she turned and led the way, swallowing to ease the dryness in her mouth and throat.

Dominic too had changed and was wearing a pair of pale jeans that moulded the muscles in his strong thighs with loving honesty, and a cotton chambray worker's shirt in the same shade of blue. Both garments were far from new; both suited him perfectly. He looked big and slightly rough at the edges, a man whose authority was effortless and unsought.

A very dangerous man, Fenella though jaggedly as she swept out in front of him.

James Maxwell was another such, but he was confined to a wheelchair. As Fenella came up he swung his head to watch her, his eyes, she saw with dismayed shock, the same green-grey as Mark's. But where her brother's gaze was open and ingenuous, his grandfather's hooded, enigmatic survey gave nothing away.

Mark performed the introductions. Very formally he said, 'Fenella, this is Mr Maxwell. My sister Fenella, Mr Maxwell.'

'How do you do.' The words came out with a slight catch that made her realise the reason for the wheelchair. James Maxwell looked her up and down with no expression; she decided ironically that his poker face was only marginally more welcoming than the hostility that emanated from Dominic.

'How do you do, Mr Maxwell,' she said, making no effort to shake hands with him in case he was not capable of it.

After a brief nod the craggy head turned to fix Mark with an inimical glare. James grunted, 'You might as well call me Grandfather. There's no mistaking your provenance.'

Dominic was nowhere near her, but Fenella thought he stiffened at these words.

'He looks like your father, Dom, doesn't he?' James went on. 'Dead spit, even to the eyes. Same colour as mine when I was his age. It doesn't need any DNA test to prove that he's one of us.'

Fenella hoped that her expression didn't reveal her astonishment as clearly as Mark's did his. Or the anger that was smouldering deep inside her at the gratuitous slur on her mother's morals.

She said crisply, 'As there was never any question but that Mark shares your genes——' of *very* doubtful provenance, her tone implied '—any talk of DNA testing is entirely superfluous.'

James Maxwell turned to look at her as though she was a small, slightly irritating disturbance. Perhaps a sandfly, she thought, trying very hard to be rational and sensible. The sort of thing you crush without even thinking about it.

'Possibly to you,' he said curtly. 'The boy's entitled to know who he is. And so are we.'

Fenella moved across to stand beside Mark, putting her hand on his arm, unconsciously massaging the tense muscles there. 'He already knows who he is,' she said quietly. 'And if you've brought him here to see how your investment is paying off, then, as you can see, it could well have the best return of any money you've ever invested.'

Mark blushed and she smiled tightly up at him, realising with a shock that in the past months he had embarked on another of his growth spurts and was now almost four inches taller than she was.

'That's if he's not been spoilt,' the old man added. He bent his fierce regard on Mark and demanded, 'Can't you speak for yourself, boy?'

'You and Fenella are doing so well that neither Dominic nor I are able to get a word in,' Mark returned politely, not in the least intimidated.

There was a moment's stiff silence, broken by quiet, apparently appreciative laughter from Dominic. 'He's got you there, Grandfather,' he said. 'I suggest you leave them both to settle in before you go into your misanthropic routine. Can I pour you a drink before lunch?'

Which revealed that the man had a sense of humour, however rudimentary and selective it might be.

Accepting fruit juice, Fenella sipped it quietly, listening while James Maxwell put Mark through a catechism on his prowess at school and his interests, hobbies and ambitions. All of which Mark answered candidly and pleasantly, without boasting or being unduly modest.

What *did* they think they were doing? Why had they brought him up here? A simple businessman's desire to see the result of an investment, or was there something more sinister in this sudden interest? She couldn't work out what they wanted, unless it really was to see if he was a suitable recruit for the Maxwell business.

In which case they were going to be disappointed. Mark had his future already mapped out, and it didn't include the Maxwells.

But James didn't actually ask the boy what he planned to do when he left school. Slowly drinking a weak whisky and soda, he encouraged Mark to enlarge on his sporting career, added a few anecdotes of his own schooldays, and then said, 'But if rugby's your game, you should have seen Dom play. Best damned fullback I've ever seen. Big enough to handle anything that came his way, beautiful hands, and a kick like Don Clark.'

Although inured to almost every New Zealander's passion for rugby, Fenella was a little startled by the fervour that rang in this Australian's voice. She looked across at the man who, long legs stretched out from the chair opposite her, drained the beer in his glass. Yes, he had the build of a rugby player, and she had had experience of the speed of his reflexes. Fugitive colour swept through her sleek skin as she remembered how that experience had been gained—and what had happened after it.

Not in the least self-conscious about his grandfather's praise, Dominic said mildly, 'You'll have Mark asking why I didn't play for the Wallabies.'

'Why not, sir?'

'Call me Dom,' he said, smiling. 'I wasn't good enough, of course.'

Mark chuckled, but James sat up and said fiercely, 'You would have been if you hadn't decided to swan off around the world. He went off for a year on a cargo ship, and when he came back decided to go to Harvard to finish off his education. Came back with a load of degrees and a whole lot of new ideas on how to run the business. By then, though, it was too late. We could have beaten the All Blacks if he'd been in the team.'

Mark cried out at this rank heresy, and within seconds he and his grandfather were deep in a discussion that ranged back through the years and the teams, each pleased to find the other as knowledgeable as himself.

Fenella hadn't been conscious of tension, but she relaxed back into her chair, only to stiffen when Dominic asked half beneath his breath, 'Were you worried that they wouldn't get on?'

Not giving an inch, she smiled into that callously handsome face and responded with bland insolence, 'Are you afraid they will?'

He showed his teeth. 'Mark is no threat to me,' he said quietly. Pale eyes flickering insolently over her, he said, 'Come for a walk.'

The abrupt command took her aback. He continued smiling in that humourless way and got to his feet, extending an imperative hand. Even as she resented her mindless acquiescence Fenella found herself rising, although she avoided that outstretched hand.

Lifting his voice a trifle, Dominic broke into the conversation. 'I'll take Fenella for a look around the garden.'

'Make it quick,' came his grandfather's growling reply. 'Lunch is in fifteen minutes.'

Dominic slanted an enigmatic glance Fenella's way. 'Fifteen minutes will be more than enough,' he said, the words a threat.

He was silent as he strode the length of the pool, not moderating his steps, so that she had to hurry to keep up. At any other time she would have stopped to admire the tropical growth, frangipani bushes with their soft flowers of cream and white and pink whose golden hearts glowed in the sunlight, and the magnificent flamboyant tree that spread over the crisp grass, its scarlet-orange flowers forming a canopy more beautiful than anything man could make.

The warm air was like a benediction on her skin, fresh yet languorous, soft with the sensitive fragrance of the tropics. Fenella was surprised to recognise quite a few of the trees and plants; coconut palms, of course, although a thousand photographs of tropical scenes hadn't prepared her for their height and grace. And there were she-oaks, wispy and familiar; later she would learn that on Fala'isi they were called ironwoods. Hibiscuses were familiar, but here they were so much larger and the flowers were perceptibly brighter than they were in Auckland. A small raspberry-coloured rose flowered triumphantly at the back of one of the borders.

Large leaves predominated, and variegation—some foliage was margined with gold, some with rose or scarlet. Everything seemed to grow in the sandy soil with unabashed lushness, from the huge salmon and scarlet trumpets of hippeastrums to herbaceous plants. Beyond the coarse grass of the lawns the thick greenery faded into jungle and mountains, green and sharp with the jagged angles that betrayed their volcanic origin, rising into the mist-shrouded interior.

Hundreds of metres across the lagoon, waves crashed into oblivion on the reef, the noise a constant vibrating roar. Against it an impassioned monologue in the local language broke out from inside the house; it sounded like the Maori she had heard in New Zealand, but was faster and a little harsher. It was answered by feminine laughter, rich and infectious.

An answering smile softened Fenella's mouth. It could be paradise here, she thought, keeping her eyes resolutely away from the resident serpent who paced noiselessly beside her until they were out of hearing of the two on the wide verandah.

Abruptly, his voice smooth and hard, Dominic asked, 'Are you happy with your room?'

'Yes, of course.' Her astonishment was obvious.

'Enjoy it,' he advised with hateful cynicism. 'Enjoy everything about this holiday, wallow in the fleshpots if you like, but don't for one moment assume that you're going to be able to rely on it in the future. If you're thinking of using Mark as some sort of lever, or as an entrée into our world, forget it. You won't get a free ride through him. Mark is one of us—you're not.'

'Thank heavens,' she said with a coolness she was far from feeling. 'I know one can't pick one's relatives, but one can feel devoutly thankful for *not* being related to certain people!'

His eyes glittered. 'Yes,' he said, as though she had hit a tender spot. Then he smiled, slow and vulpine. 'I hope you're not expecting a vigorous social life. I come here to rest, and as you can see, Grandfather is in no state to entertain.'

She nodded, molten fury temporarily submerged by compassion. 'Has he had a stroke?' she asked.

'Yes.'

'I see.' Her inward gaze brooded on the old man, a ravaged eagle in his wheelchair as he laughed at something Mark said to him and lifted a shaking hand to emphasise his own reply.

'He doesn't need your sympathy,' Dominic broke harshly in on her thoughts.

She turned her head, unaware of the way the sun conjured a silken sheen of blue on the black fall of her hair. 'Nevertheless, he has it,' she said, antagonism roughening her tone. 'But I have no intention of hovering over him like a ministering angel, if that's what you're worried about.'

'Just as well,' he returned caustically. 'He'd chew you up and spit you out if you did.'

With an effort she hoped was concealed Fenella lifted her gaze to meet his. Her eyes were very clear, the soft width of her mouth held in disciplined lines. 'Wouldn't it be better if we declared a truce while I'm here?' she suggested, aware that it was a forlorn hope yet willing to try.

'For you?' The words were a soft snarl. 'I'm sure it would be. But a truce is a little melodramatic; I don't intend to hurt you—unless you force me to. If you behave yourself you'll have nothing to fear.'

Anger irradiated her face. She said bluntly, 'I don't know what your idea of "behaving myself",' her voice invested the words with flippant scorn, 'entails, but I can assure you I don't normally hang from the rafters and beat my chest, and nor do I make it a habit to get drunk, or spit, or tell crude stories.'

'I'm sure you don't.' He even looked amused, although it didn't soften the hard-planed angles of his face. His expression didn't alter when he went on, 'Just remember that although the locals have a refreshing lack of hypocrisy when it comes to their own sexuality, they have little respect for tourists who come here and indulge themselves in a fling with any handsome islander.'

Fenella's mouth dropped open. For a charged moment she honestly didn't believe she had heard those incredible words.

Taking advantage of her astonished silence, he went on softly, 'Oh, they'll oblige. God knows, you're lovely enough to bring a dead man's instincts back to life, but they'll despise you. And it will rebound against our name.'

Her teeth closed with an audible snap. 'Perhaps you shouldn't have told me that,' she said in the tight voice of ultimate rage. 'I might think it's the perfect way to get even with a man who's humiliated me in every possible way and is now thinking up other ways to do it!'

With a smooth irresistible movement he dragged her forward so that she was standing almost close enough to touch him. His head lowered. Softly, menacingly, he threatened, 'If you do, you'll discover just how many ways there are for a determined man to humiliate a woman. And by the time I've finished you'll shudder whenever you hear the name Maxwell!'

Terrified, Fenella swallowed, her eyes darkening to the colour of midnight as they were imprisoned by the remorseless jade of his gaze. In that moment she realised how very dangerous he was, and was appalled that such a psychopath could be allowed to run around free.

'Yes,' he said with silken satisfaction. 'I mean it, every word, Fenella.'

'You're deranged,' she said shakily. 'For heaven's sake, this isn't some ancient civilisation where women were stoned to death for showing their faces outdoors! Does your grandfather realise that you're a madman?'

'I am not a madman,' he said between his teeth, dropping his hands and stepping back as though she infected him with some nameless poison. 'I am merely pointing out that it's definitely to your advantage to act in accordance with our wishes. If you do you'll not lose by it.'

She rubbed a shoulder childishly, flushing when she realised what she was doing. 'All right,' she said quietly, striving to overcome the betraying wobble in her voice, 'you've told me what you expect of me. Now, I'll tell you what I'll do. I'll do what I think is best. And no threats, no intimidation, are going to make me change my mind. I don't know why you've taken such a dislike to me, or why you think I'd be likely to sleep with any——'

'Dislike,' he said deliberately, 'is not what I feel for you. And if you can't understand my warning—think back to a sixteen-year-old girl who didn't hesitate to use her body to try to get what she wanted from a man she knew had no liking for her.'

Colour flamed indignantly across her face, transforming her into a dusky rose. '*You* kissed *me*,' she cried passionately. 'After I'd slapped your face because you insulted my mother. It was hardly an invitation!'

'You slapped my face because I made it obvious that your opinion of me didn't interest me in the least. And how is it possible to insult a woman who deliberately forced a man into a bigamous marriage by getting pregnant?' he added, contempt and distaste starkly manifested in his voice and expression.

She gasped, her eyes fixed on his implacable face. 'I don't believe a word of it!'

'Oh, that's what happened.' He showed his teeth in a smile that froze her protests into nothingness. 'If you want proof, check the dates on your brother's birth certificate and your mother's marriage lines. My father didn't want the added complication of a child, which was why you were packed off to boarding school. Your mother was, however, just a little too clever for Simon. He thought he'd have a passionate mistress waiting for him whenever he came to New Zealand, whereas she tricked him into a situation where the only thing he could think of to do was marry her. She threatened to tell my mother if he didn't. And as my mother was the one with the money, the money he spent so freely on his mistress, her blackmail worked. He was even besotted enough to forgive her for it.'

'I don't believe you,' she repeated icily, sickened by his words. 'Your father was just making excuses for his own duplicity.'

'Of course he was, but as soon as I saw your mother I realised that he'd been putty in her hands. Beautiful, a glowing dark rose of a woman with passionate allure in every movement, she couldn't have been a greater contrast to my mother, who's been an invalid for years.'

Fenella swallowed her pity and said with husky malice, 'It sounds as though my mother made quite an impression on you.'

'She did, but I'm not the weak fool that my father was. I recognised her for what she was; a sensual opportunist. I wasn't in the least surprised when she committed suicide rather than face up to rearing her son without any of the money she'd come to look on as her own. She was too old to be able to find another lover as easy to seduce as Simon, and I suppose as she had never worked in her life—unless it was on her back— she couldn't cope with the idea of going out and getting a job.'

He swept Fenella's face with a narrowed gaze that lingered on eyes flaming like dark sapphires, and her soft, scarlet, shaking mouth, before continuing savagely, 'And when I saw you, I realised you were the same sort. As events proved, I was right. You may not have started what happened, although you were certainly looking for some sort of response from me, but you participated with a far from adolescent eagerness in what followed.'

'For heaven's sake,' she said scornfully, humiliation burning circles in her cheeks, 'I was a child. I was only sixteen!'

'With a great natural talent for making love. Tell me, Fenella, was I the first man who kissed you?'

'No,' she said slowly, a reluctant honesty clashing with her instinct to tell him to mind his own business.

'And didn't you live with a man for the three years after you left school? A much older man?'

Her chin jolted back as though she had been hit. 'How did you know—you had me investigated!' she breathed, her emotions submerged in a flashflood of anger.

His eyes were merciless, as cold as the ice in a polar sea. 'Of course. Well?'

'Yes, but——'

'But he didn't count?' His sneer lacerated her emotions. 'Poor devil, I wonder if he knew that. But you got what you wanted from him, didn't you; the money to set yourself up with your friend in business.'

He was right—and yet he was wrong. Yes, she had lived with Paul Simpson, and yes, he had given her the money that had set her on her way, but Paul had had no sexual interest in women, and he had thought of her as the daughter he was never likely to have. Fenella's eyes filled with tears. He had kept the knowledge of his illness from her for the years they had flatted together, leaving her six months before he had died alone in England.

She had loved Paul as the father she had never known, and when he'd offered her a loan had accepted it with gratitude, only to discover that he had wiped the debt in his will.

'It's no use crying,' Dominic said harshly. 'Your mother tried that and it got her nowhere. I'm not susceptible to weeping women, any more than I am to your well-used, profitable charms.'

'What the hell do you mean—profitable charms?' she demanded.

'Did you think I hadn't heard? You'd been talking to your latest lover when I rang you in Auckland. "What now, darling?"' he mimicked contemptuously. 'He must be comparatively new, because he hasn't figured in the dossier. What are you going to take from him, I wonder? Money? Or have you decided it's time to settle down? Is he rich enough to keep you in luxury for the rest of your life? Or will you leave him if another, richer man comes along?'

Angrily Fenella dashed the tears away, turning so that the sun dazzled in miniature rainbows against the ends of her lashes and he could no longer rake her face with that unsparing gaze. But now, at least, she knew why Dominic despised her. He thought she was little better than a prostitute. Well, he could think what he liked; she was not going to lower herself by explaining anything.

'Obsessed with money as you are, I wonder that you let me inside your house,' she said stonily.

His smile was a masterpiece of cynicism. 'I wouldn't use you as a doormat,' he said. 'Unfortunately young Mark is fond of you. So—you stay. But behave yourself, or you'll be out so fast you won't know what's hit you.'

He paused for effect, waiting until she lifted passionately resentful eyes to meet his stare. Then he smiled with a silky menace that chilled every cell in her body, and finished, 'And the less salubrious details of your career will be passed on to him.'

Although she winced at the stark intimidation in the threat Fenella lifted her head, angling her chin haughtily. 'Mark is perhaps not quite as easily convinced as you,' she said with an icy pride. 'He knows me better.'

'He barely knows you. You were packed off to school well before he came on the scene, and since you left he's been at prep. And we've seen to it that he went on as many trips during the holidays as we could arrange. So any love you feel is damned shallow, if it exists at all and isn't merely a scheme to extend your influence over him in the hope that you'll profit from his connection with us.'

But Fenella had had more than enough. She didn't care overmuch what he thought of her, but to insinuate that she didn't love her brother was going too far.

Speaking very rapidly, she said, 'You can foul everything else with the suspicions of an extraordinarily mean mind, but you're not going to even hint such a thing. Mark is my brother, the only relative I have in this whole world. He is not a Maxwell—he bears my name and my mother's name, and I love him very much.'

'He bears your mother's name because he, like you, is a bastard,' Dominic said coldly.

She stared at him, colour leaching from her face to leave her sallow and enormous-eyed.

He watched her, his expression remote. 'Didn't you know?' he said when the moment had spun on endlessly. 'Your mother was not an original thinker; she had only a few tricks, and she tended to repeat them. She tried exactly the same scheme with your father first.'

White-lipped, she shook her head, whispering, 'I don't believe you. How dare you say that?'

'Because it's true.'

'Oh, no,' she said quietly, recovering her composure. Scorn rang in her clear voice; she faced him down. 'You're lying. My mother told me about my father. He was much older than her and he died fairly soon after they married. They lived in Dunedin. He was an orphan, like her. After his death she came up to Auckland because she liked the climate better.'

'She lied. Oh, come on, Fenella, you must have known,' he said, the words snapped out with curt impatience as she continued shaking her head. 'When you applied for your passport you would have had to supply your birth certificate and a copy of your parents' wedding certificate. Which does not exist.'

She bit her lip. 'My mother got my passport for me eight years ago,' she whispered. 'When I went to Tahiti on a school trip.'

'I see.'

She looked up and saw him looking at her with something like sympathy, the barbaric lines of his features almost compassionate. Somehow, she knew then that he was telling the truth. Her mother's tales of that brief doomed marriage had all been lies. In a voice that quivered she spat, *'Don't you pity me!'*

He had long lashes, thick and straight and dark. They drooped, hiding his emotions except for a gleam that could have been anything. 'Why should I pity you?' he said. 'The fact that your parents weren't married has nothing to do with you.'

'You just believe that it makes me behave like them.' A little colour seeped back into her skin and her voice. She was discovering that anger filled the empty hole in her heart more than satisfactorily.

The broad shoulders moved in a shrug. 'You made me believe it when you made love to me like a houri.

And when you moved in with a man old enough to be your father only a year later.'

Oh, Paul, she thought sadly. You were the only father I did have, ever.

Her shoulders straight, she flung at him, 'So what does that same reasoning make you? A man perverted enough to be aroused by a child!'

The moment she said it she knew she would have done better to remain silent, but even so she hadn't expected such a vicious reaction.

Dark blood rushed along his cheekbones; his mouth straightened into a thin hard line as he snarled, 'No, damn you, not then, not ever. Oh, I wanted you, but you were no child! You knew just how to push the buttons, and, young as you were, you looked and behaved like a woman of the experience you've just admitted you'd had.'

Too alarmed by the conflagration she had caused to tell him that her 'experience' had involved a few shy kisses from boys of her own age, Fenella said quietly, 'I don't think this conversation is getting anywhere, and I'm sure it's more than fifteen minutes since we left Mr Maxwell and Mark.'

Those narrowed eyes scanned her face, moving with deliberate slowness from her eyes, darkened to navy blue by the effort of keeping her composure, down the thin straight line of her nose to her mouth, wide and set, for once alarmingly pale beneath the defensive coat of lipstick.

Fenella stood very still, staring down into the heart of a golden allamanda in its nest of glossy leaves, confident and brash in the hot tropical sunlight. From one of the trees a dove crooned, the little sound making her feel a long way from home. She could feel the track of his eyes, yet in spite of everything, she couldn't summon the will to move.

'Fenella,' he said quite gently.

She looked up, her mouth trembling beneath eyes dense with shadows.

'I'm sorry,' he said unexpectedly. 'I thought you knew.'

'Did you? I find that very difficult to believe,' she replied with bleak resistance as she turned away. 'Anyway, it doesn't matter.'

CHAPTER THREE

THE OTHER two were still discussing rugby, apparently not missing them at all. However, Fenella noticed the keen look that James Maxwell gave her, as though he and Dominic had discussed beforehand what should be said, and he was checking her reaction.

The thought of the most intimate details of her life being pawed over by these two made her feel sick, but she stiffened her shoulders and threw him a level, unyielding glance. He looked blandly back, shrewd eyes enigmatic in the old face.

Nothing, she vowed as they moved inside to the cool dining-room, absolutely nothing the Maxwells could say or do was going to hurt her. She was only here to make sure that they didn't hurt Mark. What they thought of her was immaterial; after all, they couldn't feel any more contempt for her than she did for them!

As for what Dominic had told her—she would not think of it at the moment. She needed to collect her thoughts in privacy before she could face the implications.

Lunch was served on the terrace, shielded from the intense rays of the sun by a creeper with white flowers and a sweet, potent scent. Fenella looked out across the swimming pool to the mountains, still cloaked in their wrappings of cloud.

It was a perfect setting for cane chairs with big green and white striped cushions and a round table also made of cane with a glass top. Hibiscus flowers lay in an artfully contrived heap of glowing silken colour in the middle of the table, and as a background there was the muted roar of the waves on the reef. The food was simple but excellent: iced avocado soup with fresh-baked bread, a salad with cold roast chicken, and fruit and cheese to follow, the apricot flesh of ripe paw-paws glowing against the icy green of kiwi-fruit from New Zealand and the soft pink slices of mango.

James Maxwell ate sparingly, watching with amused interest not unmixed with respect as Mark put away his usual enormous meal. It seemed that he had decided to approve of his younger grandson.

Hurt and angry, Fenella tried to convince herself that this was a good thing. After all, Mark was definitely a Maxwell, so he was entitled to whatever the other Maxwells had. On the other hand, she didn't know what payment they would extract for the privileges they might offer. All she was sure of was that there would be one. Neither of these men struck her as being unduly generous, and she suspected that *quid pro quo* could well be their motto.

Her mouth tightened as she drank a cup of excellent coffee. Whatever, they would find that she was not so easily disposed of. Mark was her brother and she had his best interests at heart. Not for anything was she going to abandon him to them, with their dispassionate businessman's attitude to life.

James Maxwell broke into her thoughts by asking conversationally, 'And what do you do for a living, Fenella?'

Startled, she searched Dominic's swarthy face, seeing nothing but indifference. Apparently his grandfather didn't know he had had these illegitimate relatives investigated.

'I draw houses with pen, ink and watercolours,' she said after a second, transferring her gaze back to the older man. He lifted an eyebrow and she smiled tigerishly. 'People like pictures of houses that are important to them,' she explained. 'I produce them.'

He looked astonished. 'You earn your living from that?'

'Oh, yes, I do quite well.'

Mark said proudly, 'She did one of the old admin block at school for our retiring headmaster; he said it was the present he liked most.' He grinned admiringly across at his sister. 'It only took her a day or so.'

'How do you go about it?' James Maxwell asked.

His interest seemed quite genuine, so she relaxed a little. 'Normally I take a photograph to work from at home.' She judged his expression correctly, saying crisply, 'Yes, I know the purists sneer, but I don't claim to be anything more than an illustrator, and my clients want a record rather than a work of art.'

'As well as drawing, you own a share in a florist's shop, I believe,' Dominic said smoothly.

She shrugged, lapis lazuli eyes narrowing infinitesimally. 'Yes. A friend and I are partners. We work from her garage in Parnell, so there's no rent and we can sell flowers much more cheaply than most. We're doing quite well.'

'They do flowers for special occasions,' Mark informed them with pride. 'One of my friend's mother always gets Anne and Fen to do the flowers for her special dinner parties, and so do lots of other people. They're very good. Fen gets the ideas and Anne does the technical bits. When a sheikh from some Middle Eastern country came out to New Zealand there was a big reception in Auckland, and Fen and Anne did the flowers for that too. They were in all the newspapers.'

'Won't your partner miss you? Christmas must be one of the busiest times for florists, surely,' Dominic remarked, the deep, beautiful voice bland as cream, stroking along Fenella's raw nerves like an opulent fur.

She sent him a sizzling smile. 'Oh, she agreed that I had to come. Fortunately her daughter is off school for the holidays now and is every bit as good as I am at the technical bits, so she'll help with the Christmas and New Year rush.'

'And of course you wanted to spend Christmas with Mark,' Dominic said smoothly.

'Of course,' she agreed, daring him to go any further.

Mark chuckled. 'Poor old Anne has to do the buying, anyway. Fenny finds it awfully hard to wake up in the morning, you have to shout in her ear and shake her, but even when she's on her feet and functioning she doesn't actually know what's happening until about nine o'clock. She can look you straight in the face and not know who you are.'

'Hey, that's not fair!' she protested, smiling in spite of herself. 'I'll admit I'm not at my best in the morning, but a cup of tea or coffee usually sets me up.'

She hated Mark giving away small details of her life; it made her feel naked, exposed to a prurient gaze. But of course Mark, although not insensitive, had no inkling of the state of affairs between her and Dominic Maxwell.

He laughed at his sister's slightly flushed cheeks and went on teasingly, 'And you can conduct a conversation with her in the middle of the night, tell her things, even ask her questions and get a proper answer, but she'll be sound asleep, she won't remember a thing about it the next morning. Weird, isn't it?'

'You normally discuss things with her in the middle of the night?' Dominic was leaning back in his chair, his pale eyes hooded as they rested thoughtfully on Fenella's face. She felt the impact of his scrutiny like a blow.

'When I was a kid I used to sneak into her bedroom in the middle of the night and talk to her, just for fun, but now it's only when I come in after the pictures.' Mark grinned ingenuously. 'I tell her I'm home and she asks me whether it's been fun, and we discuss things a bit, although I know perfectly well I'm going to have to go through it all again next day!'

Dominic raised an infuriatingly quizzical brow. For some reason Fenella felt heat flash along her cheekbones, her embarrassment exacerbated by the ambiguous smile that touched his hard mouth for a moment. She didn't know what he was thinking, but she knew she didn't like it.

'That's enough,' she said to Mark, a slight edge to her voice revealing that she meant it. 'Don't go blurting out all my idiosyncrasies!'

He looked mournful. 'You mean I'm not allowed to tell them that you have the sort of temper the Vikings would have respected?'

She grinned. Her placidity was notorious. 'Not unless you want to rouse it,' she said sweetly.

'Not a word shall pass my lips,' he swore, pretending to be terrified but looking inordinately pleased with himself.

Fenella noticed that both the Maxwell men were watching them with something of the interest of a palaeontologist confronted by a new and exquisitely interesting fossil. The intense survey sent tiny cold footprints of unease along her nerves. Hadn't they ever seen a brother and sister teasing each other before? Or were they looking for something else, a weakness they could capitalise on?

If so, in whom?

Her lashes shaded her eyes as she finished the coffee in her cup; once she peeped through them to find Dominic's gaze still on her, the harshly striking features impassive, belying the very real intelligence she knew he possessed. That poker face must come in very handy in boardroom dealings, she decided, trying to overcome the hollow feeling in the pit of her stomach.

She failed, of course, for the feeling was fear, and she had every right to be afraid of these two men. They had proved themselves to be ruthless and unstoppable in both their personal and business lives. If they decided she needed to be crushed, neither would hesitate for a moment.

But how could they crush her? she thought, rallying to scoff at her wild imaginings. The only thing they could do was lure Mark away, and she wasn't afraid of that. He too possessed some of the Maxwell obstinacy and persistence, as well as a loyalty that could come as an unpleasant shock to them.

Of course, they had already seen some evidence of that trait in his insistence that she come to Fala'isi with him. And in spite of Dominic's cynical suggestions, she loved her brother and knew it was reciprocated.

'... normally have a siesta.' The old man's rumbling voice broke into her thoughts. 'Feel free to follow my example if you wish.'

A small fair man of indeterminable middle age, wiry and bland-faced, came on to the terrace. A nurse-cum-valet, Fenella decided, noting the air of quiet professional competence. He was introduced as Peter Brown, and nodded politely to them all before wheeling Mr Maxwell into the darker reaches of the house.

Fenella got to her feet. 'I think I'll rest too,' she said a little too quickly.

Mark began to follow her. 'I'll come and see where you are,' he said, obviously eager to talk things over. Then he hesitated, good manners driving him to turn back to Dominic. 'Unless you have anything for me to do?' he asked a little diffidently.

'Not today.'

Grinning, Mark rejoined Fenella. She had been standing with her face averted, but as she turned to go she cast a swift glance up at Dominic's face and saw there a dark confidence that chilled her soul.

But she managed to talk easily to Mark as they took the way back to his bedroom, a pleasantly masculine room two doors away from hers. It too had its own bathroom and dressing-room, and in between, so he informed her artlessly, was Dominic's room.

Firmly repressing a secret shiver down her spine at the thought of Dominic sleeping through the wall from her, Fenella led Mark into her quarters.

'Hey, this is nice.' He looked around with open admiration. 'My room's very luxurious, but not like this. What do you think of them?'

'The rooms? Very comfortable, like an upmarket hotel.'

'No, twit, the Maxwells! My grandfather and Dominic. Do you like them?'

'Not a lot,' Fenella admitted, sinking down into the white upholstery of the armchair. 'But they've both been polite.'

'You're my sister,' Mark said quietly, his green-grey eyes stubborn.

She was touched. 'Yes, I know, but I'm not related to them. Anyway, it doesn't matter what they think of me, or I of them. The important thing is that you get to know each other.' She spoke with an emphasis that caught Mark's attention.

He nodded, watching her with an oddly adult look in his eyes. 'I know—that's why I came. I'm glad I did. I didn't know that Grandfather had had a stroke. Do you think that's why he asked me?'

'It's possible.' She leaned back against the chair, tilting her head so that her hair flowed in a theatrical flood of heavy black satin over the chalk-white fabric. 'Ah, that's better. Heavens, but it's hot, isn't it? You have a right to know who your relatives are. If you like each other, and there's no reason why you shouldn't, that's a bonus.'

'They'll like you, too,' Mark predicted confidently. 'For a sister you're not such a bad old egg, you know.'

Laughter swelled, free and unforced, from the slender olive length of Fenella's throat. She reached up to push the clinging cloud of hair away from her damp temples, murmuring demurely, 'You're so kind, sir.'

Something prickled the length of her spine, setting a million small sensors alive with alarm. She froze, her eyes fixed on Mark as he looked towards the wide glass doors out on to the terrace. His eager smile told her immediately who stood there.

'Hi, Dominic. Are you looking for Fen?'

'No, for you.' The deep smooth voice was completely toneless, not a hint of emotion colouring it, yet Fenella sensed strong emotions held in check by an indomitable will. 'I'm taking the chopper up and I wondered if you'd like to come.'

Very carefully, so he wouldn't see her fingers tremble, Fenella released her hair and sat back in the chair, trying to keep her face expressionless as she turned it towards the door.

Looming against the blaze of the sun outside, Dominic was a combination of grace and massive strength. A shiver of apprehension ran through her. Touching her tongue to suddenly dry lips, she thought fancifully that he looked as Hades must have appeared to Persephone when he came to drag her off to his underground kingdom: terrifying, merciless, all-powerful, a dark raider from the nether reaches of a nightmare.

Mark's face lit up. 'Yes, I certainly would!' But he hesitated, looking at his sister.

She forced her insouciant grin. 'Not for me, thank you.'

'I didn't think you'd want to go,' Dominic said easily. 'You appeared to be a nervous flier.'

'She's not, really.' Gallantly Mark leapt to her defence. 'She just isn't all that confident in helicopters.'

'A pity,' Dominic said smoothly. 'I'll see you down at the pad in five minutes.'

When they had both gone, Fenella relaxed, her breath whistling out from strained lungs. She was going to have to stop being so absurdly conscious of the man! He knew it too; she had recognised the small grim smile as he stood silhouetted against the tropical afternoon light, intimidating her with his very stillness and size.

Furious with herself for sitting around brooding about Dominic Maxwell and his unnerving effect on her, she got up and put on a bathing suit, a tank-suit of shocking pink lycra that clung to her full breasts and narrow hips as affectionately as a lover. What she needed was some exercise.

The water in the pool was lukewarm but refreshing. Fenella enjoyed swimming, loved the sensuous stroke of the water over her slender curves, the caress of it in her hair streaming out behind her in an inky cloud, the smooth stretch of muscles and sinews as she unkinked a body that had travelled through the atmosphere and into yesterday since her very early awakening that morning in New Zealand.

She didn't pull herself out until the noisy chop of the helicopter began to drown out the thunder of the waves on the reef. Even then, it was without undue haste that she donned the thick white towelling wrap she had found on the back of the bathroom door.

With it was an exquisite silk satin robe of exactly the same pattern, its edges piped in silver. Fenella had held it to her face, smiling at the smooth slide of the material across her skin, but it had to be so expensive that she decided then and there she was never going to wear it.

The towelling one was quite a different kettle of fish. It was going to be very useful. For one thing, it covered her right down to her knees! Fenella pushed her wet hair back from her slender neck as she strolled past clumps of shell ginger, admiring the delicate pink and white arcs of the flower heads against the vivid stiff leaves. A bird called, soft and compelling, not at all like the drowsy cooing of the doves.

Eyes softened by dreams, revelling in the sweet warm air, jungle-scented, salt-sharpened, she gazed at the jagged spires of the mountains. As she watched the clouds swirled apart to reveal yet more peaks, sharp as a serpent's tooth, stark spears of glistening rock where waterfalls hung suspended until they were hidden once more by clouds.

An odd sensation, of belonging, of coming home, made her catch her breath. Turning away from those frightening peaks, she looked across the lagoon, her gaze captured by the glittering, dancing surface of the water. A canoe balanced by a small outrigger swooped across the dazzling sea, bound for one of the tiny *motu* on the outer edge of the lagoon, a small island completely covered with vegetation where coconut palms bent down over incredibly white coral sand.

A kind of ache, a pang of delight mixed with a poignant sadness, washed over her, held her motionless. She thought that some kind of spell was being woven about her, sweet yet perilous.

So this, she thought a little tremulously, is the fabled lure of the South Pacific!

As the helicopter's engines died she almost ran into her room.

Of course, by the time she had showered and pulled on a white sleeveless jump-suit she had regained her composure, rationalising away that eerie moment of revelation as just another manifestation of jet lag.

Fastening the halter-neck top at the waist with its three buttons, she surveyed herself in the mirror, wondering whether the deep neck was too *décolletée*. After a moment her wide shoulders lifted in a small, insolent shrug. She wasn't actually showing anything beyond a slight occasional curve, and then only when she moved. And if it upset either of the Maxwell men, no doubt they would let her know! It was ridiculous to let them make her paranoid about her wardrobe and her body.

Donning sunglasses to hide her eyes, she wandered out on to the terrace, following her ears to Mark's voice as he gave someone—presumably his grandfather—a rundown on the ride.

'Dom says he'll teach me how to navigate,' he was saying excitedly. 'And then perhaps how to fly it!'

She couldn't hear his grandfather's reply, but the tone sounded approving.

'Well, it's very kind of him,' Mark said cheerfully. 'Even if he has got nothing else to do these holidays! He's a brilliant pilot, isn't he? We swooped around those mountains as though we were on an eagle!'

He leapt to his feet as she came around the corner of the terrace, but, before he could begin to tell her of his experiences, Mr Maxwell intervened to command him to get his sister a drink. Fenella accepted a glass of pink nectar, pleasantly cool with a faint bitter tang that was more refreshing than any sweetness could be.

She was sitting with her back to the house, listening to Mark wax lyrical about his flight, when some alteration, some impalpable tension in the atmosphere, tightened her shoulders.

'That's enough, you'll bore the ears off everyone,' Dominic commanded, and Mark laughed and subsided, his reluctance plain but his manners forbidding any further excesses of enthusiasm.

'I hear you're going to teach the boy how to navigate,' James Maxwell remarked as Dominic sat down beside Fenella.

'If he wants to learn.' The smooth voice was faintly satirical.

Mark grinned but said promptly, 'I do.'

'And if Fenella doesn't mind, of course.'

Startled, she looked up, her gaze captured by the opaque pale jade of his. Without need for reflection she said, 'No, of course not.' She had no need to think about it; Mark would be safe with this man.

Dominic's dark brows lifted and the smile that didn't soften the hard beautiful line of his lips turned sarcastic. 'Then that's all right,' he said calmly, and without missing a beat turned to his grandfather and began to speak of something that had happened in the stock market in Melbourne.

Not for long, however. The conversation drifted to the state of the economy, and thence to politics, and Fenella was astonished to realise that she was being encouraged to give her own views, as was Mark.

It was oddly exhilarating. Neither Maxwell gave quarter, and she found herself having to defend her point of view with great vigour, and even once admitting that it was wrong! However, she was pleasantly surprised to discover that for all their autocratic exteriors neither man was intolerant of views different from his own, and both listened to what Mark had to say with a respect that wasn't, as far as she could see, feigned.

She also realised, with a sinking feeling in her stomach, how awesomely intelligent Dominic was. As well as impressive powers of reasoning and logic he had a sharp incisive ability to pick out the weak points in any argument, and was quite merciless in attacking them.

Now she understood how he had turned his grandfather's national construction firm into a worldwide super-conglomerate of vast wealth and many strings to its bow. The aura of power that had struck her even in that first meeting seven years ago was definitely earned. And yet, she decided warily, stripped of everything, the gloss of fortune and power, the smooth sophistication and education, Dominic Maxwell would still draw the eye, for it was the steel in his character that made him the man he was.

A truly frightening adversary.

And until she knew exactly what the Maxwells had hoped to gain from this holiday she would have to consider both men her enemies.

The freewheeling discussion was interrupted by a pretty Polynesian girl bearing a tea-tray. James insisted that Fenella pour, a duty she managed without spilling anything, and when the little ceremony was over Mark demanded she come for a swim with him.

'Whereabouts?' Dominic asked lazily. 'Pool or lagoon?'

Mark shrugged. 'In the lagoon. I'd rather swim in the sea than in any pool.'

'OK.' His half-brother stood in one smooth powerful movement. 'I'll come with you.'

Fenella's mouth dried. Without thinking she said, 'I won't——' then stopped, the words drying up in her mouth, because Dominic had turned the cool shimmering gaze on to her and she couldn't go ahead and say that in that case she wouldn't join them.

A tiny half-smile curled his enigmatic mouth. He said nothing, and she floundered, 'I've already been in once——'

'Yes, but only in the pool!' Mark scoffed. 'Where's your sense of romance, woman! You can swim in a pool any time at home, but you're not likely to have the opportunity to swim in a tropical lagoon very often.'

The only way she could retrieve the situation was laugh and pull a face a him, and say comfortably, 'As ever, small brother, you're right. I'll meet you on the beach.'

It took her a little longer to struggle into her already wet bathing suit, and she didn't like the way the material showed every line and curve of her body, but she told herself she was being idiotic; she had worn the thing in public before and never been embarrassed by it. Still, she hauled on a large white shirt over her suit, glad she had decided to bring it as a cover-up. Although perhaps she should wear the towelling robe; the shirt revealed the full length of her long tanned legs.

Stop it! she adjured herself ferociously. Who cares if Dominic looks at your legs? Plenty of other men have seen them, and there's nothing wrong with them!

Lawns spread down towards the coarse white coral sand of the beach, the grass bordered by coconut palms and shrubberies arranged in such a way that it was almost impossible for anyone to see the house from the beach. Clearly the Maxwells liked their privacy.

In spite of the struggle with her bathing suit Fenella was the first to arrive, so she waited in the shade of the palms, her eyes fixed firmly out to sea, admiring the many hues of the lagoon, from palest jade the colour of Dominic's eyes at the water's edge to a deep glowing blue in the centre. Butterflies lurched about in her stomach; to calm them she stared at the little *motu* across the lagoon almost directly opposite the house, admiring the way the palms formed an airy canopy above the thick, shaggy vegetation.

Her fingers itched to get it down on paper or canvas, even though she knew she would never be able to do it justice. Normally she accepted the limitations of her small talent without pain, but occasionally she longed for some touch of genius so that she could express the aching joy the scene gave her.

'The tiny island of Motuiti,' Dominic's deep voice informed her. 'The name means little island. We lease it from a Fala'isian family in Avanui, the village in the next bay. You probably noticed the houses as we flew in.'

Without turning, yet so conscious of him that the skin pulled tight between her shoulderblades, she said, 'Yes, I did. What do you use the island for?'

'Nothing. We have the occasional picnic there. But it faces straight on to us.'

'So you made sure no one could overlook Maxwell's Reach.'

'Yes.' It was surprising that there could be such a threat contained in his deep tone. 'We value our privacy.'

'And,' she countered with a snap, 'you can afford to buy it. Lucky you!'

Not in the least affected by her retort, he replied with cool insolence, 'Yes. Actually, there's very little we can't afford to buy.'

And that was a threat too. Sorely tempted though Fenella was to state that neither Mark nor she was for sale, she resisted the impulse. It would be, she decided rapidly, counter-productive. It was best to slip as easily through this situation as she could.

So she allowed amusement to colour her voice as she murmured, 'Ah, that must be one of the pleasures of being rich.'

'Yes,' he said with utterly infuriating self-possession. 'Unfortunately, with the means to gratify almost any desire comes the realisation that most are not worth appeasing.'

And what on earth did he mean by that? With an odd dislocated feeling, as though they were conducting two entirely different conversations, she ploughed on cheerfully, 'Never mind. Over-indulgence is supposed to be bad for the character, so it's just as well you've decided not to go in for it.'

'Is that why you've lived more or less like a nun since your first lover died?' His voice was even but deliberate, insultingly detached. 'Did over-indulgence surfeit you of the pleasures of the flesh? I'd have thought a man so much older than you would have slowed down in bed.

Or perhaps he wasn't a particularly good lover, and you only stayed with him because he was rich.'

Fenella swung around and looked up into the brutally handsome face, her own stormy with suppressed emotion. 'Mind your own business,' she said icily.

The broad shoulders, sleek and bare and powerful, a glowing copper in the light shade of the coconut palms, lifted in a shrug. 'Some might think it is my business,' he said quietly, his eyes never leaving her face. 'After all, Mark is my half-brother too. His moral standards are my concern.'

Scorn hardened the contours of her face. 'What contemptible hypocrisy!' she said swiftly. 'I suppose the women whose names have been linked with yours over the past few years have all been delivered to their front doors with a chaste goodnight kiss? No one knows that Mark is any relative to you, so what difference can his moral standards make?'

'For all the world knows, or will ever know,' Dominic returned, his eyes never leaving her face, 'a chaste goodnight kiss is all that any woman has ever had from me. I don't flaunt my hormones around for the gutter Press to point the finger at. As for Mark—do you really think he's going to remain incognito for long? He looks like us, and when he's seen with us, sooner or later someone is going to ferret out his identity.'

'Then, so that you don't have to worry about his morals, or lack of them, why not leave us alone?' she flashed. 'After all, you've managed to do that very successfully for the last seven years.'

'And run the risk that you'll take the sordid little story of his conception to the newspapers? No way, lady. For better or for worse, he's a Maxwell. While he was a child he was safely out of sight, but it's not going to be long before he's out in the world. We need to know what sort of person he is.'

'So that he won't shame the glorious name of Maxwell?' Outrage and anger made her foolishly reckless. 'I shouldn't think he'd be able to shame it any more than your mutual father managed to do.'

There was a fraught silence, so tense that Fenella's eyes widened as she stared up into the bronze mask of his face. Fear, thick in the base of her stomach, drove the colour from her face as she marked the leaping savagery in his expression.

'And your slut of a mother,' he said, his lips barely moving. 'And you, living openly with a rich man more than twenty years older than you. What kind of woman does that?'

One who wanted a father, she could have said. One who needed the uncomplicated affection Paul had offered, affection without strings, his only recompense the pleasure of her company, and the delight of teaching her all the things she had never learned at school, for he had been a born teacher. It was thanks to Paul that she was able to talk knowledgeably about art and music, about the history of the Pacific and the methods Chinese painters had used to achieve the incredibly sophisticated effects of their silk scrolls. Paul had taught her so much...

But she couldn't tell this man that. She held her ground, her head lifted, her long neck aching with the effort of keeping it rigid, and said calmly, 'The kind of woman who loves her brother and is prepared to fight for him. That's all you need to know about me, Dominic high-and-bloody-mighty Maxwell.'

'I'll have to find out whether that's true, won't I?' His mouth eased into a cruel smile, enjoying her bewilderment. 'Or whether you too can be bought for the right price. On past evidence, I'd say you can.'

Her eyes narrowed, but before she could speak Mark's voice interrupted the spell of tension and she turned towards him as he loped up to them, her shadowed eyes half covered by her lashes, her expression stringent with composure.

'Got a good covering of sun-cream on? Right, then, let's go,' Dominic said in his normal voice, clearly not at all affected by the ugly little exchange. 'Just pace yourself—the water is warm, and can be enervating. Don't swim too far.'

Naturally athletic, Mark was an excellent swimmer, but he took heed of the caution and spent the first minutes trying out his paces, diving to the bottom to look at the shells and the corals, persuading Fenella to float in the warm transparency of the water and look down at the ever-changing patterns that the sun on the surface made on the bright bottom. If Dominic hadn't been there, looming in her consciousness like some dark shadow, she might have soothed her jangling nerves enough to enjoy herself.

But every time she pushed the curtains of dark hair back from her face she saw him, a being powerfully sculpted from copper, the strength implied in his bearing and physique more than affirmed by the effortless ease of his swimming. As he cut through the water, sea-water darkened the charcoal-brown of his head, glistening over the swarthy copper skin, formed the smooth coating of hair across his chest into a pattern as old as humankind.

Fenella tried to keep her eyes away, but imperceptibly they found him again and again, noting the tight line of buttocks, the swell and play of sleek, powerful muscles, the overwhelming physical dominance as he ate up the distance.

'He must have swum for miles,' Mark suggested later in the tropical night when he came to collect her for dinner. Hero-worship shone from his features, altered the timbre of his voice. 'Gosh, I've never seen anyone power through the water like that, without making an unnecessary ripple, even.'

'Oh, well, Australians are practically born in the water,' Fenella said flippantly, trying to hide her uneasiness. 'Look how well they always do in the Olympic Games in swimming. Gold medals by the ton.'

He grinned. 'I hope some day I can go for as long as he does. He told me that's how he keeps fit. He doesn't run, although he plays tennis. I'll bet he's good at that too. He's going to give me a game tomorrow morning before the sun gets up high. Did you know there's a tennis court here? They must be really rich, mustn't they? I mean, super-rich.'

Fenella nodded, adding fairly, 'But from the little I've read, they work very hard for it.'

Mark dismissed this with a shrug. 'You have to work hard for everything, otherwise it's not worth it, is it? I'm going to be the best surgeon that it's in me to be.'

As always when he spoke of his ambition, his voice was matter-of-fact. And as always when she heard him, Fenella prayed that nothing would come between him and the fulfilment of his desire.

'Keep that thought in mind,' she said, smiling, because when he spoke she could see the man he was going to be, and realised that Dominic was right: there was little of his mother to be seen in his face. He was all Maxwell, from the incipient size of him to the sculptured lines of jaw and forehead and cheekbone, and the bluntly beautiful features.

Even his colouring was like his grandfather's; when James Maxwell had been Mark's age he would have had the same chestnut hair and steady green-grey eyes. Dominic's bronze skin and unnerving jade regard must have come from his mother.

Dragging her mind away from the recollection of the blaze of pale colour in those eyes when he got angry, she twirled and patted the white evening culottes beneath the cotton jacquard vest of the same colour, asking, 'How do I look?'

'Nice,' Mark said matter-of-factly. 'Just right. I like those big silver balls dangling from your ears. *Very* chic! And the silver sandals too. Did you buy them flat so that you wouldn't be any taller than me? 'Cause if you did, it was wasted. I've left you well behind!'

She grinned and gave him a swift hug. 'No, I just liked them.'

'You could wear heels as high as anything and still not reach Dom,' Mark said artlessly. 'He must be at least six feet four, mustn't he?'

'Well, six foot three, anyway.'

'How about me? Are these clothes all right for dinner? You don't think I need to put my blazer on, do you?'

He wore grey slacks and a white shirt and looked just right for what was probably going to be a more formal dinner table than he was accustomed to.

'You look perfect,' she said, draping a white georgette scarf around her shoulders and hoping fervently that she was right and neither Maxwell was dressed in bright aloha shirts and shorts.

She had been right. James Maxwell had on a light linen jacket, but Dominic wore a superbly tailored shirt over equally well cut slacks in linen. Neither she nor Mark possessed clothes with such expensive tailoring or superb fabrics, but her instincts had been correct. While the ambience was hardly formal, it was definitely more so than dinner on a summer evening at her flat!

It should have been the sort of evening magical memories were made of. Outside was the warm tropical night, sweetly scented and mysterious, where stars trembled against the black velvet sky and the sound of the waves on the coral reef was an unchanging ever-present but muted roar in the background.

The dining-room was cool and luxurious with a fan spinning above the table and white linen setting off the wonderful meal. Crystal and silver gleamed and winked, and orchids glowed with exotic beauty in the centre of the table.

They were served oysters with caviar and champagne vinaigrette, 'from the lagoon,' Dominic told Mark. And yes, sometimes they had pearls in them, superb golden ones.

'About the colour of your sister's skin,' he drawled, fixing Fenella with an assessing stare that made her skin prickle unnervingly. He grinned as Mark poked eagerly around in his. 'It's no use looking, any pearl will have been found long before they reach the table,' he said. 'If you're interested we'll go out one of these days and look at the beds.'

'Oh, yes, I'd like that!' Mark plied Dominic for more information, listening enraptured as the deep voice told one or two tall stories about the pearl fisheries on the island.

Fenella kept her face expressionless, but her unease deepened, for there was no doubt that Mark was indulging in a full-blown case of hero-worship, and no doubt that both Dominic and James Maxwell were encouraging it. She could only feel that it was a sinister development, but instinct warned her that as yet she had no defences against it.

She would have to wait and see exactly what they were up to.

Beef served in a spicy Oriental sauce followed the oysters, and for pudding there was a fresh fruit salad, the delicious, exotic flavours melded superbly together. Afterwards, when she and Dominic had coffee and James Maxwell drank tea, she was offered a liqueur. Dominic said nothing when she refused it, but she was not surprised when he too declined. She had noted that he drank as sparingly as she did of the wine at dinner.

Afterwards James commanded Mark to follow him to a billiard table in some other region of the house so that they could play pool. Left in uneasy proximity to Dominic, Fenella got to her feet.

'I'll go to bed now,' she said calmly.

He looked at her with coldly amused eyes. 'Very well. I'll see you in the morning.'

Not, she thought austerely, if I see you first. Her soft red mouth stretched into a smile that had nothing of its normal infectiousness, she walked stiffly out of the room.

CHAPTER FOUR

OF COURSE Fenella woke early the next morning, stretching in the big bed as the sun rose up behind the mountains, setting fire to a bank of high clouds. *Red sky in the morning, shepherd's warning.* Did that apply to the tropics, where there were no shepherds?

But of course summer was the rainy season here, the time of tropical cyclones with their awesome devastation. Not every year, of course, and from recollection very few hit Fala'isi.

Fenella wriggled and yawned, trying to drift back off into blissful oblivion. To no avail. Now, when she had a rare opportunity to sleep in, her body obstinately demanded that she get up and do something!

Muttering grumpily, she pushed back the sheet and wandered into the bathroom. After a quick shower she pulled on a pair of shorts and a brief cotton top. The sun had just broken free of the mountains when she walked swiftly down past the pool and across the wide lawn to the bank above the beach. The lagoon was dappled with pink and red and grey, a sheet of mother-of-pearl beneath the already warm rays of the sun. The light on the water reflected up against the smooth hull of the big cruiser, transforming the white surface into ripples of colour like watered silk. Sitting down under a coconut palm, Fenella leaned back against the grey smooth trunk, watching with dazzled eyes.

She had hoped to use this time for thinking about the revelations made by Dominic the day before, and her own reactions to them, but she was too enthralled by the magnificent subtlety of the dawn. And by the time it was over, by the time the colours had faded into the blue and green and white of daylight, people began to

68

appear from behind the headland that sheltered the village of Avanui. Clearly the locals rose with the sun too, and accomplished as much as they could before the heat of the day.

Several people walked past, calling to each other, laughing, their brown faces strongly marked with the heritage of Polynesia.

Smiling, Fenella said, 'Good morning,' and they answered in English, looking at her with a friendly curiosity that wasn't in the least offensive.

A small boy toddled up and beamed at her, teeth flashing in his little brown face, his eyes merry and mischievous as he proffered the core of a shell, burnished by the waves to a sinuous curve of nacre.

'Thank you,' she said, and on an impulse dropped into his chubby little starfish hands the flower she had picked on her way down, a pink and white blossom of shell ginger, shaped like a cowrie and as smoothly polished.

He grinned again and, holding it carefully, dashed unsteadily back to his family, who were smiling a few yards away.

'You staying with Mr Maxwell?' a handsome youth asked, his dark eyes not at all bashful as they wandered over her long legs.

Fenella smiled. 'Yes. Are you all from Avanui?'

He nodded and took a few steps towards her, stopping suddenly as his gaze moved to a point behind her. 'Oh, hello, Mr Maxwell,' he said, his eyes dropping hastily in a way that she knew meant respect.

Dominic's voice was cool and perfectly friendly. 'Hello,' he said, then repeated the greeting in the Maori tongue of the island.

The little group beamed at him, and chorused a greeting, the older ones, Fenella was surprised to hear, calling him by his first name as though they knew him well. Clearly, however, they put him on a pedestal. The respect in their faces and voices was easy to discern.

To her astonishment and chagrin he leaned down and caught her by the hand, effortlessly drawing her to her feet before urging her down on to the beach and introducing her to everyone, keeping her left hand in his as she shook hands around the group and tried to memorise their names. He knew them all, even the girls who hung bashfully back and the children who called out to attract his attention.

And they knew him, their dark eyes resting thoughtfully on the fingers held so mercilessly within his, their broad smiles flashing with amused understanding.

After the first instinctive tug for freedom Fenella gave up, the only sign of her anger and chagrin the dusky colour lying in a wash over her high cheekbones.

At last, after handing over a brilliant red fish for his grandfather, the islanders left. This time when Fenella pulled away Dominic loosened his fingers, setting her free. She stepped back, demanding curtly, 'What on earth was that in aid of?'

'You looked as though you were getting quite friendly with young Sia.'

Memories of his voice warning her against any romantic entanglements with the locals resounded tauntingly in her brain. Contempt flickered, coldly blue, into her eyes. 'I don't make a habit of having affairs with boys many years younger than I am.'

'No,' he returned with soft hateful effrontery, 'that's a pleasure you reserve for men many years your senior. Men who can pay your price.'

Biting savagely into her bottom lip, she turned away from that unyielding gaze. She was not going to explain why she had lived with Paul, nor justify herself. Let him think what he liked!

'You'd better get that fish into the fridge,' she said frigidly, 'before it goes off.'

'I'll be back in five minutes.'

When she made no reply he hooked a finger underneath her chin, tilting her mutinous face so that he could scrutinise it. A sharp sizzle of awareness, as painful as an electric shock, raced from the point of contact to every nerve in her body. Fenella's eyes widened; helplessly she stared into his antagonistic gaze, imprisoned by the touch of his finger, her breath coming swiftly and painfully through lips that were soft and scarlet beneath transparent gloss.

Infinitesimal muscles tightened over the strong framework of his face, bringing the brutal features into prominence. His mouth hardened and through the darkening jade of his eyes there crept a bleak anger.

Yet he did not let her go. It was as though he too was held in thrall to the violent enchantment. Fenella heard the sound of the waves of the reef, felt the flower-laden breeze caress her, but she was only aware of the copper mask of his face, the features drawn in some unbearable need.

'No!' he said violently, the normally beautiful voice harsh and impeded. 'I won't go that way again!'

The savage words gave Fenella just enough strength to pull jerkily away. Dragging in a painful breath, she rested her forehead against the bole of the palm while she fought to regain some sanity.

'Don't touch me again,' she said at last, hating the thinness of her tone yet unable to overcome it.

'You needn't worry. You sully my hands.'

She waited until he was out of sight before racing back to the sanctuary of her room as though all the devils in hell were after her.

After that it was sheer torture to have to go along to breakfast, torment to sit opposite him in the glorious morning light and pretend that nothing had happened. He, she noted sourly, seemed to have no such problems. He even smiled at her with a deceptive charm she bitterly resented, and asked her how she had slept, as though he had never touched her, never mortally insulted her.

She wondered if she was the only one to be aware of the seething undercurrents of tension, but a glance at James Maxwell convinced her that she was wrong. He was watching her from beneath lowered eyelids, and as she met his gaze it flicked for a second to Dominic and back to her.

Yes, he could read the situation, and he was not happy about it. Not nearly as unhappy as she was, she thought grimly.

Fortunately Mark was entirely unconcerned, his cheerful early morning exuberance the only thing that stopped the meal from being too ghastly to bear. He decided to spend an hour with Dominic learning the basics of navigation, and then he'd go swimming, and perhaps today he would go fishing...

'What are you going to do?' he asked, turning to Fenella.

She smiled, shrugging. 'I might do some sketching.'

'Or perhaps you could go into Fala'isi,' Dominic suggested, watching her with hooded eyes. A cruel taunt needled through the words as he drawled, 'The shopping is excellent there.'

Fenella gave him a set smile and responded calmly, 'I don't think so, thank you. It seems a pity to spend any time in a city; one is very like another, isn't it?'

'Don't you like shopping?' he asked, apparently idly, still watching her as he leaned back in his chair, tone and actions at variance with the purpose she felt radiating from him.

'Well, yes, but——'

'Perhaps you need some money,' he said courteously. 'I'm sure we can arrange something. We can't have——'

'No, thanks!' she broke in, outraged by his offensive crudeness.

He shrugged, not in the least intimidated, or even affected by her anger. 'Or you could just book your purchases up. We have accounts at most of the stores.'

Not trusting herself to speak, Fenella shook her head.

Mark was looking at her anxiously and for his sake she stayed silent, unable to give Dominic the roasting he deserved. Who the hell was he, to show his contempt so clearly? He knew nothing more of her than what he had learned from some sleazy enquiry agent, and he dared treat her as though she could be seduced by offers of money!

Still seething, she finished her coffee and got to her feet. 'I'll go for a swim, I think,' she said austerely, and left, her back poker-straight as she walked away.

Her bed had been made, the bathroom tidied, and the clothes she had worn yesterday spirited off, so there was nothing she could do there to take her mind off the hateful man. With gentle fingers she touched the smooth petals of the moth orchid, her expression gradually easing from turbulence to serenity.

After all, what did it matter that Dominic thought she was the slut he had called her, a mercenary, promiscuous female with her eye to the main chance? She thought worse of him. And she didn't care. He might look like something dreamed up by a fevered romantic and possess the virile masculinity of a splendid animal and an effortless authority, but he had a mind like a sewer.

She wanted him.

Her forefinger hesitated on the smooth white petal, then fell to her side. She stared sightlessly down at the delicate flowers above their glowing bowl.

There. She had admitted it, the secret hidden under the anger and the hatred and the scorn. She wanted Dominic Maxwell.

But she was not going to succumb to a passion that had all the elements of one of Nature's nastier jokes. When she made love, it would be with a man who valued her, who was prepared to give her tenderness and affection as well as sex. Making love with Dominic might have all the awesome force of a tropical storm, but like a cyclone it would only leave her broken and battered. His passion would be fundamentally destructive.

And, she thought with a faint sigh as she straightened, she had seen just what could happen when you gave in to passion like that. Her mother had killed herself rather than live without it.

For of course she did not believe Dominic's assertion that it was the prospect of having to earn her living that had made her mother commit suicide.

Nor did she believe that her mother had deliberately set out to seduce either her father or Simon Maxwell into marriage by becoming pregnant. Or, she thought painfully, perhaps there had been no marriage; perhaps she was illegitimate. Her mother would not have been the first solo mother to lie to her child, painting a rosy picture of an essentially unromantic situation. That was understandable, whereas the thought of her deliberately bearing children to use as a bargaining counter with her lovers was not.

To start with, she had not been a maternal woman. Oh, she cared for her children, but, looking back, Fenella thought that most of her mother's love had been poured out on to the man in her life. Even with Mark, whom she had adored, she was curiously distant.

Fenella's mouth softened into a smile as she remembered how she used to love caring for her little brother when she came home for the holidays, and how her mother had always been eager for her to do so.

The smile faded as she recalled the way her mother had waited for Simon during his long absences, longing for him, living for the day when he returned to her. When he did, she had glowed like a lovely incandescent rose.

So Dominic was wrong. Her mother might have been weak, but she had truly loved.

And she was not going to repeat her mother's mistakes by falling in love with a man who was ultimately not worth her love. Simon Maxwell had betrayed her mother; Dominic would not betray her because he would make no promise of eternal love. If he felt anything for her it was the same basic desire she felt, the simple uncomplicated need to mate.

Which, she thought with irony, was probably by far the safest thing to feel. If she let him get near her emotionally the result would be shattering. Desolation.

Her expression settling into lines of determination, she reached down and took her sketch pad and pencils from the drawer, and went out on to the terrace. Fala'isi was not to blame for Dominic's cruelty, and she wanted to make a record of its transcendent beauty.

Fenella chose a spot on the terrace, framing her sketch in the creeper with the waxy white flowers, which she now knew to be stephanotis; beyond it lay the pool and beyond that the peaks of those incredible mountains. Her fingers flew as she got the basics of the sketch down on paper, but slowed as she began to flesh the picture out with detail and texture.

When she had finished, she moved closer to the creeper so that she could study the flowers. The perfume floating on the drowsy air was sensuous yet oddly fresh, as befitted, she thought drily, its use as a bridal flower.

She was striving to render properly the leathery sturdiness of the oval leaves when she was conscious of another presence. She knew who it was, too.

Perhaps if she kept on working he would go away. With fingers that were kept steady only by an intense effort she shaded in a portion of stem.

Dominic said, 'Do you ever wish you had more than a talent?'

Forcing her voice to remain wooden, she replied, 'Occasionally, but genius asks too high a price. I'm not dedicated enough. I enjoy what I do, I do it to the best of my ability, and I know that I'll never be more than a competent draughtswoman.'

'You're young to have such a cool, critical appreciation of your own standard of aspiration.'

She shrugged. 'I had help. Paul taught me most of what I know. He wasn't into false praise.'

The deep voice altered subtly. 'Ah, yes. He was quite a connoisseur of the arts, I believe. Did he see himself as a patron?'

'I think he did, in some ways.' Yes, her voice was cool and remote, no hint of emotion. Fenella was rather pleased with her control.

'A teacher, perhaps, too?' The question hung silkily on the scented placid air.

'Yes, he would have been a good teacher. But most of all, I think,' she said, suddenly unable to bear the inquisition any longer, 'he saw himself as a father.'

There was a moment's silence, as though she had managed to shock him. Then he said in an arrested voice, 'I see.'

'I doubt if you do. Paul was the kindest man I've ever known.' Fenella stood, gathering her sketch pad and pencils, her hands trembling as much as her voice. She had to get away before she broke down entirely, yet, desperate as she was, she couldn't leave it like that. 'He didn't ask much of me and I gave him that willingly, because he gave me so much more. I hope I made his life a little happier than it would have been otherwise. He was a good man.'

'A good man, to use your need for a father figure to lure you into his bed?'

Oh, he was quick, and she had given too much away. Without looking at him she said tonelessly, 'I thought you'd decided that I was the one who lured him into a relationship.'

'I did. However, I believe you when you say he gave you what you were looking for—security, I suppose, and a father figure to fill a gap.'

Exhausted, she said, 'You seem to know all about it.'

'But you're not going to confirm or deny.' His voice had hardened, the momentary softening gone. 'I can't work out whether you're a hard little bitch with an eye to the main chance, or just a pathetic little scrap with the sort of background that makes you ideal prey for a man who offers security for you and your brother.'

Sheer fury, the like of which Fenella had experienced only once before, spurted like fire through her, galvanising her action. But this time she knew better than to hit him.

She swung away, her face flushed with the force of her rage, and spat, 'I've never heard anything so in-

sulting in all my life! I'm no poor little scrap, you pat-
ronising great oaf! I'm in control of my life and that's
the way I like it, and you have no right to go rooting
around through my past, trying to fit me to your cheap
theories! I told you about Paul because he was a good
man and doesn't deserve to have your contempt,
although God knows, he wouldn't have cared! He was
too confident, too sure of himself, too aware of his
strength to worry about what others thought of him.
Now take your muddy mind and get out!'

Someone called his name.

'Mark,' she whispered.

A searing, hooded glance, then Dominic turned and
strode across the terrace and into the blazing light of the
sun, its rays warming the charcoal hair to faintly glowing
embers.

When Fenella reached for the back of a chair her hands
were trembling so much she couldn't grasp the cane.
Limply subsiding, she drew a deep breath, and another,
forcing herself to smooth over the jagged edges, to claim
her racing pulses. It took all her knowledge of medi-
tation to summon up some form of composure, and even
then she felt as though she had been caught in the eye
of a cyclone, that deceptively quiet area in the midst of
unbridled destruction.

But what shocked and dismayed her most of all were
the secret but unmistakable signals from her body.

Furious, hurt, disillusioned although she was, she was
aroused.

It seemed that she was just as vulnerable to his erotic
charisma as she had been when she was sixteen and he
had kissed her as though she were a fully mature woman.
In spite of his insults, her hand stole guiltily to touch a
mouth throbbing with the forbidden desire that first
furious kiss had roused, never to be quite forgotten.

Perhaps it was because of that kiss that she had never
made love with anyone else. Paul had said she was naturally fastidious, and she was, but she suspected she
would have experimented more if Dominic hadn't

somehow impressed her with an indelible stamp of possession.

For a moment she allowed her mind to wander in delicious erotic byways, until with a sick shame she dragged it back to the present.

Shaken by the unnerving confrontation, she wandered, sketch pad in hand, around to the lagoon side of the house. Perhaps she could ease some of her turmoil by trying to convey the lazy, sparkling ambience of the lagoon on to paper. It might help to further calm her shattered nerves, she thought with a humourless little smile.

The sound of Mark's voice, eager and uninhibited, lifted her head; with a kind of fatalistic resignation she saw him and Dominic, clad only in trunks and sunscreen, walking down to the beach several yards away. Her eyes dwelt hungrily on the rippling muscles of Dominic's shoulders and back, the spare narrow line of his hips and the long, heavily-muscled thighs.

Oh, God, she thought suddenly, I should get out of here as fast as I can!

An eager desire heated her body, from her prickling skin right down to the individual cells. A strange pulling sensation in the pit of her stomach made her squirm with frustration.

Angrily she returned to her sketching. But Mark's voice attracted her attention again. Slowly she peered from beneath her lashes. They were setting up a wind-surfer down on the crisp white sand, and it was obvious that Dominic was explaining how to sail it. Beside it was another.

Fenella bit her lip. The Maxwells could give Mark so much more than she could. Oh, she did her best, and she was managing, they certainly weren't poor, but there was no way she could afford to buy him something as sleek and frivolous as the brilliantly coloured board and sail down on the beach.

And while it was easy enough to say righteously that money wasn't everything, somehow the maxim didn't seem to apply to a much-loved younger brother who deserved all she could get for him.

The sun beat down on the two dark heads, Mark's chestnut, Dominic's unusual shade of warmed charcoal as they put the windsurfer in the water. Mark yelled in sheer exultation as the wind caught the sail, and Dominic pushed the other one in and leapt on to it, chasing him. Catching up within seconds, he took up a position alongside Mark, encouraging him, as much a master of the skittish board as he would be of any other sport.

Fenella's trained eyes appreciated the sight they made, two sleek male animals, then turned inwards to imagine Dominic on a horse, his strong legs clamped around its body. From there she drifted on to imagine him lean and dark and dangerous on skis, and finally as a nude in the life classes she had taken...

Gulping, she dragged her mind back to the beach. Mark let out a great whoop of delight, and the other surprisingly carefree laughter had to be Dominic's. With a shock of astonishment Fenella realised that it was the first time she had heard it.

Pushing down the thought that it would be heavenly to have him laugh with her like that, she abandoned her sketch pad and pencil and settled to watch, chin on her knees, arms entwined around them.

The brightly coloured sails swooped and spun over the translucent waters of the lagoon, darting between the big cruiser and the shore, making frequent forays further out. Occasionally the blue sail with Mark beneath it collapsed into the water. Each time Fenella jerked up, watching with anxious eyes, but he always managed to raise it, and before long the intervals between one capsize and the next had lengthened perceptibly.

It was an idyllic scene, Fenella thought sadly, her gaze following a small canoe until it landed on the sparkling beach of Motuiti, then watching with awe as the huge rollers swept down the reef in a flurry of spray and confusion. Paradise.

She was sitting on the terrace with James Maxwell when they arrived back, slicked with salt, Mark's nose and lips covered in bright yellow zinc ointment, his expression one of unalloyed joy.

'Well, I can see you liked that. How did he go?' James asked Dominic.

'He'll do. A few more hours of practice will see him competent enough to go out on his own. We'll be ready for lunch in ten minutes.'

He didn't even look at Fenella. Telling herself she was relieved, she waited until they had disappeared before saying, 'I thought I heard something about a cyclone on the radio this morning.'

James grunted. 'Yes, Ola is mucking about there somewhere, wondering which island he's going to hit.'

Expecting him to laugh, she told him about the red sky that morning, but to her surprise he nodded. 'It can be a bad sign. There are others too. Heavy swells with nothing to account for them, wind from an unusual direction, perhaps a sheet of cirrus clouds when you wouldn't expect one. The islanders know, although they can be wrong. But I don't think Ola's going to come this way. Fala'isi does get the occasional one, but for some reason it seems to be off the track of most of them. Not worrying about it, are you?'

Smiling, she shook her head.

'Well, we're not likely to get into trouble even if the eye passes over us. The house is built to resist cyclones.' Pride crackled through his gruff voice. 'It's the end result of years of research. Dominic started it; decided that it was too bad to let you New Zealanders get away with building all the cyclone-resistant houses in the Pacific, so he set out to capture as big a slice of the market as he could. He's done well. We're selling the technology all around the Pacific and in some parts of Asia too.'

Fenella tried not to look too interested. 'Most of the villages seem to have thatched roofs here, although I noticed one or two iron ones from the helicopter.'

He nodded. 'Thatched ones are more appropriate for the climate, but they're a hell of a lot of work to build and maintain, and they don't last in a cyclone.'

Dominic came out on to the lanai; he had apparently overheard the last few sentences, for he said easily, 'No, but they don't kill anyone in one either. All the materials are here for repair, and they don't cost much. They're cool in the heat, and weatherproof. However, it takes a lot of time and effort to make and erect them, and iron roofs are fashionable.'

Carefully keeping her face blank, Fenella allowed herself a small sideways glance at him. He was fully in control, his expression calm and no more than mildly interested. Repressing an odd little shudder down her spine, she said, 'But of course you'd rather they built the houses your organisation has designed.'

The wide shoulders lifted in a small shrug. 'That's up to them. We're not in the business of persuading anyone to do what they don't need to do.'

'If you're interested,' James Maxwell said, smiling slyly at Fenella, 'you should get Dominic to take you over to Avanui. Some of the houses there are the traditional type and some are more modern, ranging from concrete block affairs with corrugated iron roofs to the ones Dominic's been advocating, blocks made of the local soil highly compressed and dried, with thatched roofs. Their new meeting centre is reinforced concrete block; it should stand any number of cyclones.'

'What about cyclones?' Mark said eagerly as he joined them. 'Are we going to have one?'

Both men grinned, but when James told him there was not likely to be one, his disappointment altered both smiles to a certain grimness.

After that the days seemed to pass like honey pouring from a glass, sliding smoothly from beautiful dawn to sleepy noon and thence to sensual night, days when the frigate birds swooped and wheeled over the little *motu*, nights when tiny frogs sang their exotic songs in the trees outside.

Fenella and Dominic maintained a truce of sorts, neither relaxing but both making some effort to keep the peace, a truce that was all the more necessary for being so fragile. Occasionally she looked across at him and saw a trace of savagery in his expression, but that iron will kept it well disciplined.

Sometimes she wanted him so much that the faint masculine scent of him set her heart beating wildly, her control crumbling. But she banished her aching hunger to the furthest recesses of her heart, endeavouring for Mark's sake to be her normal self.

For Mark was enjoying himself immensely. He told Fenella that if all his teachers were as patient as Dominic he would get straight 'A's all the time. As this was more or less his usual position in class Fenella was inclined to dismiss his praise, until she joined them one day when Dominic was explaining some particularly tricky piece of mathematics to his half-brother.

Then she saw what Mark meant. Surprisingly forbearing, Dominic explained again and again, using different approaches and examples, until at last Mark grasped it. Fenella realised that Mark was right; his half-brother possessed far more patience than the virile exterior would lead one to believe.

It was that evening that Dominic said to her, 'I gather Mark is top of his class.'

'Yes. But surely you get his reports?'

He nodded, watching Mark and James play the game of chess which had become a nightly ritual.

'Yes. I've never been particularly interested before.'

Her hackles rose, but before she had time to respond scathingly he resumed, 'Has he any idea of the direction he might go when he leaves school?'

Fenella sent him a swift searching look. 'Yes.' She added after a moment's hesitation, 'I'm surprised he hasn't told you.'

Without removing his eyes from the other two he asked blandly, 'Jealous, Fenella?'

She began to deny it hotly, then fell silent. Honesty compelled her to admit, 'Yes, I suppose I am.'

'You'd be unusual if you weren't. You needn't worry; he's absolutely devoted to you. Any hint of criticism and he comes bristling to your defence. I have to admire his loyalty.'

She refused to rise to his bait. Silence stretched tautly between them.

He broke it by asking quietly, 'What does he plan to do with his life?'

Surely it couldn't hurt to tell him. 'A doctor,' she said, adding, 'A surgeon, really. One of his school friends has a mother who's a brain surgeon, and that's what Mark wants to do.'

'Is it a real vocation, do you think, or merely a response to an admired woman?'

'More than that, I'm sure. He's always been interested in medicine, but the brain surgeon bit is fairly recent. He gets a kind of—glow about him when he talks about it.' Her eyes dwelt on Mark's face, softening as he grinned cheekily at his grandfather. 'I hope he makes it,' she said softly.

'There's no reason why he shouldn't. He's an extremely intelligent boy, and he's got all the perseverance in the world. Look how he's learnt enough Maori to be able to converse with the boys from the village.'

'He's good at languages,' she said absently. 'He came home today and said that one of the elders—Pihaia, I think, the old fisherman with white hair—is taking some of the boys to an island to collect a certain sort of shellfish.'

'Yes. The shellfish produces a red dye that's used to colour *tapa* cloth. The village has hereditary rights to gather it from one of the atolls about twenty miles from here, and Pihaia takes the boys there every year. It's a kind of initiation process. They all enjoy themselves immensely and come back convinced they're men.'

She nodded.

'What's the problem?' he asked shrewdly.

'I think Pihaia must have said something to Mark about going.'

His brows shot up. 'I see.' He too looked across at Mark. 'If he has, it's a great honour.'

'Well, yes, but you know Mark, he can charm the birds into his hands. He's only fourteen, but I notice the girls watch him——' She stopped, scarlet-faced, because Dominic was chuckling.

'Boys grow up early here,' he said. 'And so do the girls. And they have a refreshing attitude to sex, quite without hypocrisy.'

'He's too young!'

'I'd have said myself that he's an extraordinarily mature fourteen-year-old.'

'It's all very well for you,' she said fiercely, keeping her voice low. 'I suppose you indulged yourself up to the hilt. What if——' she blushed but carried on manfully '—if he does—and if—what if there's a baby?'

'I'm glad to hear that you're so responsible, but the women here learn from their mothers how to prevent unwanted children.'

'I suppose you know all about that too,' she snapped.

'There are no children running around here with my features,' he said, feral mockery gleaming in his smile. 'And if you're trying to discover whether I played with the girls, then the answer is yes. But I don't now, haven't for years. And we remain friends. If Mark does lose his virginity here, it will be with much more grace and considerably less guilt and recriminations than if he bedded a girl in New Zealand.'

Her cheeks were fiery red, but she ignored her horrified confusion and said stonily, 'Possibly. However, if Pihaia does suggest that Mark goes with them, do you think he should go?'

'My advice would be to let him go. Pihaia's been taking boatloads of boys for years——'

She looked at him sharply. 'Did you go?'

'Yes.'

Fenella brooded for a moment, then looked up, meeting his eyes frankly. 'I worry about him,' she said simply.

She managed to stop herself from saying 'he's all I've got' but she knew he had heard the unspoken words. Annoyed at giving him the opening, she braced herself for another hateful insinuation about using Mark as her entrée into the Maxwell world of money and power, but for once he passed up the opportunity. She knew better than to think that it was because he had changed his mind about her, but common sense told her that it was probably because they were sitting close enough to the other two for any altercation to be heard.

'I know. I even find it understandable.'

She shrugged a little impatiently, her eyes wandering back to where Mark was shaking his grandfather's hand and promising to give him a better run for his money the next night.

The man beside her said, 'Do you ever do portraits?'

'I have done, although I'm never satisfied with them. Why?'

'I'd like to give Grandfather one of Mark for Christmas.'

Fenella lifted her brows, smiling ironically at the suspicions she had harboured when she had first arrived here. How melodramatic they seemed now! James Maxwell had been badly frightened by his stroke and decided to make a neat ending to all the knots left unravelled in his life, one of which was Mark. And because Dominic loved the old man he had encouraged this meeting.

Now, she thought, both men liked Mark for what he was.

'I could try,' she said thoughtfully. 'Mark doesn't like to sit still, and I probably won't be able to catch that—that open charm that's so special to him, but I'll give it a go.'

'I'll pay you, of course.'

She stiffened. 'I wouldn't dream of it. It can be some small recompense for your hospitality.'

'The hospitality is actually Grandfather's,' he pointed out, his expression enigmatic.

Her chin came up and he laughed softly. 'All right, Fenella, I know your views on accepting money from me.'

Startled, she looked up at him, met laughter and something else, something that was gone too quickly for her to recognise in his eyes. Colour rushed through her skin. 'Good,' she said in a gruff voice. 'It was a bloody insult, and you meant every word of it.'

'Yes, I did.'

She knew it was stupid, but she couldn't stop herself from asking with more than a hint of belligerence, 'And do you still think I want to use Mark as a way to find myself a rich boyfriend?'

His expression was enigmatic. 'I believe you love him,' he said. 'But even so, you could still have a hidden agenda, couldn't you?'

Well, what had she expected? He was a cynic through and through, and it was ridiculous to feel disappointment like a crippling blow to her body.

CHAPTER FIVE

NEXT morning when she brought in the early tea Mari surprised Fenella by asking her to be ready to go across to Avanui with Dominic after breakfast. The house-keeper had become more friendly, although her dig-nified reserve prevented any overt familiarity. It was useless for Fenella to tell herself she was stupid to be so chilled by the older woman's determination to keep her at a distance, because Mari certainly wasn't like that with the rest of the family. Her attitude to the Maxwells was one of unawed respect, and Mark had completely won her over; she spoiled him shamelessly.

'Is it about the trip to the island?' asked Fenella, still uneasy about Mark's part of it.

Mari smiled. 'Yes. It will be fun for Mark, he'll enjoy a few days away just with the men, and Pihaia will tell him things no woman is allowed to hear.'

From the faint twinkle in her eye and the primming of her mouth, it was fairly clear that the women knew exactly what information the old man imparted to his charges.

'He's your uncle, isn't he?' asked Fenella.

'Yes, my mother's brother.'

Fenella, sitting up in the bed, pulled the sheet up with her to her throat. Since the first night she had slept naked for coolness, but she was bashful enough to cover herself when the early morning cup of tea arrived.

'All mothers,' the housekeeper pontificated, 'whether of birth or of care, find it hard to cut the ropes, but boys need to grow up and become men.'

On which piece of philosophy she sailed out of the room.

It was easy enough to say, Fenella thought crossly. Of course she knew she had to cut the apron strings, but paddling twenty miles across the Pacific in an outrigger, even if it did carry an engine for emergencies, seemed a fairly drastic way of doing it.

What if a cyclone came? Ola might have finally blown itself into one of the vast unpopulated areas of the Pacific where it could do no damage, but that didn't mean another storm wasn't gathering strength in the devils' kitchen where they were brewed.

Of course, most of them didn't come to anything, and those that did usually waited until after Christmas.

How about tidal waves?

Or waterspouts, she thought, disgusted with herself. Why not the Great Sea Monster? Or even an iceberg, for heaven's sake; it was almost as likely!

Pihaia's boat had a radio, and no doubt he used it to listen for the weather forecasts. He could summon help the same way. Any danger, and even if for some reason they couldn't paddle the canoe they'd be back in the six hours it took the outboard engine to get them home. Or, in the case of a real disaster, Pihaia could summon Dominic in the big cruiser to bring them all back.

The chill crawling down her spine had to be stupid nerves, and the sooner she conquered them, the better.

So when she and Dominic walked over the headland to Avanui on its wide bay Fenella was composed and calm, ready to give assent, if that was what was needed.

She had been to the village several times, once with Mari who showed her her house and introduced her to her three married children and several vigorous grandchildren, and twice with Mark, when she had been greeted with the easy friendliness she had come to expect from all the islanders but Mari. This time, clearly, was a serious occasion, for everyone was gathered in the big meeting place. Fenella was glad she had worn a skirt and blouse, and remembered Dominic's instructions not to sit with her feet pointed towards anyone.

They were met by a formal deputation and festooned in flowers, Dominic's a chiefly loop of ferns and frangipani around his neck, hers an exquisite string of some dark red flower, one she had never seen before. The woman who put it around her neck said something in a voice that was clearly provocative, and Dominic grinned, pale eyes dancing as he replied. Fenella wished she understood the local Maori language, for his answer sent them all into gales of laughter. Guiltily, she decided that as soon as she got back to New Zealand she was definitely going to take Maori lessons as, with a song and a wave-like movement of dancers, they were conducted to the place of honour.

As it happened, she, Dominic and the chief had chairs, so she didn't have to worry about the direction of her feet. Everyone else sat on magnificent *tapa* mats made by the women from the bark of the paper mulberry tree, the terracotta colour of the precious dye blending in with the blacks and browns that formed the main colouring.

Straightening her spine, a little self-conscious at being so much on display, Fenella listened as the chief let it be known to his people that Pihaia was not averse to taking Mark with him that year. Her eyes wandered around the villagers, vivid in their brightly coloured cottons with wreaths of flowers in their hair and around their necks, frangipani, hibiscus, the sweet-scented native gardenia, many she didn't recognise. The exquisite star-shaped flowers in her garland were, she noted, confined only to the young women. Perhaps only unmarried women wore them.

There were many speeches, some formal and of high oratory, some that made everyone, including Dominic, rock with laughter. At the end, Pihaia stood up and gave what Fenella concluded was an undertaking. He finished with a dramatic gesture towards a small group who were sitting behind the main line of villagers, and she looked over and saw Mark, unusually solemn, with some of the boys from the village.

Most of them she recognised; they had spent many hours with Mark on the beach, a cheerful, almost cheeky tribe, buzzing with high spirits. They were serious now, dark eyes fixed on their mentor as he spoke.

He finished, and there was silence. Dominic said something to a distinguished old man who had been sitting a little behind him. Getting to his feet, the man, a chief by his bearing, spoke at some length, again gesturing at the boys, who looked self-conscious. He was answered by the man who had begun the speeches. Another silence, during which everyone looked thoughtful until someone broke into song, which was caught up by everyone there. The women remained seated, but the men leapt to their feet and began what looked to be very similar to a *haka*, a war dance. To Fenella's astonishment, Mark joined in, acquitting himself very well, if the smiles and murmurs of appreciation were anything to go by.

When this was over, the women sang by themselves, gradually joined by the men as they simmered down from their energetic and threatening postures. The melody was sweet and complicated, the harmonies too intricate for Fenella's untrained ear to decipher, but the women's high voices soaring above the rich deep tones of the men produced an odd quiver in her stomach.

That seemed to mark the end of the formal part of the ceremony. The official party got to its feet. Noticing that Fenella was a little uncertain, Dominic held out a hand to her; she saw grins break out all over as she took it, and flushed when she realised that he had reinforced her supposed position as his lover.

'Who was the man you spoke to?' she asked under her breath to hide her confusion.

'He's my talking chief.' He grinned as her brows shot up and explained, 'A chief doesn't talk, it's beneath his dignity. So we have talking chiefs who do the work for us. It's a convenient system; if anything goes wrong it's the talking chief's fault, whereas we're able to claim the credit when everything goes according to plan.'

'I'll bet it's not quite like that,' she said disbelievingly.

'Well, that's a simplification. A talking chief is in a position of great responsibility. In the old days he was immune from all acts of war and aggression; they acted much as heralds did in the Middle Ages.'

They were being escorted past the big hall to a long row of mats sheltered from the sun by a thatched roof on a framework of poles. Fenella murmured, 'What happens now?'

'Like all good get-togethers, it ends in a feast.'

The feast was served immediately, arriving in containers woven from the fronds of the pandanus tree. This time everyone sat on the magnificent mats; by now it was extremely hot, so Fenella was grateful for the roof. It didn't actually make things cooler, but at least it kept the direct rays of sun off her head.

She ate sparingly, listening as Dominic and the chief and elders discussed matters affecting the island. They spoke mostly in Maori. The women served the meal and only then sat down to eat, the one next to Fenella being the chief's big dignified wife.

'Eat some more,' she urged, when Fenella showed signs of slowing. Meekly Fenella took some more delicious fish and began to nibble on it.

The chief's wife grinned. 'One meal won't make you as big as I am,' she said.

Fenella flushed. 'I didn't—I wasn't thinking that.'

Rich laughter greeted this. 'I know, I'm teasing you. Lucky for me that our men like their women big. You come from Auckland, don't you?'

'Yes, I do.'

'Ah, I did my nurse's training in Auckland. Still as cold as ever in the winter?'

Fenella chuckled. 'It must have been a great shock to you! Compared to this, anywhere would be cold!'

'I never got used to it, I was glad to come back home. How long are you going to be here?'

'Until the end of January, I think. Mark goes back to school then.' Fenella looked over to where he was laughing with his friends as he tucked into an enormous meal and added wryly, 'That's if there's enough food on Fala'isi to keep him.'

'Ah, it's good to see them eating well. He's a nice boy, Dominic's brother.'

Fenella smiled, her heart warming to the open uncomplicated praise. The red flowers around her neck gave off a delicate perfume. Her fingers delicately stroking the lovely blossoms, she asked, 'I haven't seen these flowers before. What are they called?'

'*Tiare aloka*—the flower of love,' the older woman translated. 'It only grows on Fala'isi, and only in the bush. If you dig it up and plant it in your garden it dies, every time. But it grows well beside the streams up in the mountains.'

'Why is it called the flower of love?'

The older woman's face crinkled into laughter. Leaning forward and dropping her voice, she confided, 'The scent's supposed to have strong aphrodisiac qualities.'

Fenella swallowed. 'Really?' she said faintly.

'Yes, but it's very subtle in its effect. It won't make you leap into bed with the first man you see, like a witch's love potion. It's obvious that you and Dominic want each other, but Mari says you aren't spending the nights together, so we decided perhaps you needed some help.'

Fenella ducked her head low, unable to hide the great tide of colour that rose as high as her forehead. 'I see,' she said in a strangled voice.

The chief's wife roared with laughter and patted her hand. 'Don't worry, we're modern, sophisticated women, we know perfectly well that a pretty little flower isn't going to set your hormones racing through your blood. It's just a bit of fun.'

Fenella didn't need any outside help; her hormones were in a constant state of ferment. Her appetite gone, she looked down at the beautifully arranged food in an endeavour to conceal her misery.

'You have to do what you think is right,' her companion said shrewdly, obviously aware of the hungry turmoil Fenella tried so hard to hide. 'There is always a choice. When my mother told me I was to marry Tama, I could have run away with another man. It would have shamed my family, but I could have done it. At the time I didn't know Tama very well, but,' her eyes twinkled, 'I liked the look of him, and I decided he would do very well. And he has.'

Her gaze was amused but affectionate as it rested on the bald head of her extremely dignified husband. Fenella envied her that love, and the certainty that came with it.

Shortly after that it was time to go home. Walking along the track worn by Mari and the maids as they went back and forth to their homes, Fenella filled in a silence that threatened to become uncomfortable by saying, 'That was interesting.'

'It was a form of indemnity insurance,' Dominic told her casually, holding back an intrusive branch.

'What?'

He looked down into her puzzled face. 'If anything goes wrong—well, we were told of the disadvantages as well as the advantages. We can't cry foul and demand reparation. I think the custom of taking reparation for a wrong was known to the New Zealand Maori as well.'

'*Utu*,' she said absently. She stopped and looked up at him, searching for reassurance in the strong features, her eyes smoky with doubt. 'Nothing will go wrong, will it?'

'Don't be stupid, Fenella! Of course something could go wrong. Just as something could go wrong here, or in the main street of Auckland. We live in a dangerous world, and we're fragile.'

His impatience and her foolishness made her grimace. 'I'm sorry, I'm just being stupid,' she sighed, setting off again.

'Given that, though,' he said drily, 'everything that can be safeguarded will be. They're no more eager to die than Mark is, and they've been sailing these seas with singular success for some thousands of years. You should worry a little less than when you see him cross a street in Auckland.'

She smiled a little forlornly. 'All right, I'll be sensible. When do they go?'

'Tomorrow.'

'What will he need to take?'

'Fenella,' he said crisply, 'he knows what he has to take. We'll provide him with the food he needs, which isn't much because they'll be eating off the land—or the sea, in this case.'

She nodded, determined not to show any more foreboding. In a voice that was casual and cool, he said, 'By the way, a New Zealand opera singer is coming to the Opera House in Fala'isi for a concert in two days' time. Would you like to go?'

She hesitated. She was asking for heartbreak, she knew it, but she said, 'Yes, I'd love to,' just the same. Then she did a double-take. 'Fala'isi has an opera house?'

'Mm-hm. Not very big, but the acoustics are excellent.'

'It must be the only one in the Pacific Islands.'

'I think it is. We'll go out to dinner before the concert. You haven't really seen any of the island yet.'

'What I've seen has been enough,' she sighed. 'It must be one of the most beautiful places on earth. I can see why the first explorers here thought that the Pacific Islands were some kind of earthly paradise.'

'Yes, indeed.' But he sounded aloof suddenly, the precious moments of closeness banished as though they had never existed.

Still, the active antagonism he had displayed earlier in the holiday seemed to have vanished, and although she didn't allow herself to make too much of this truce, she found herself watching him through her lashes, trying to see through the gladiator's mask to the man behind, so much more complex than any gladiator had ever been.

Mark left at dawn the following day in an outrigger that barely managed to fit in the five excited boys and the old man. Surveying the flimsy vessel with its noisy crew, Fenella felt a recrudescence of her anxiety, but everyone else seemed perfectly happy to see them set out, so, swallowing her fears, she listened with a carefully tranquil face to the small ceremony held in the light of the sun as it rose over the mountains.

The chief spoke; someone said a prayer, and everyone sang a hymn, then the boys, sober now but unable to hide their anticipation, said their goodbyes.

Eyes gleaming, Mark kissed Fenella goodbye and shook Dominic's hand, said gruffly, 'Look after her, won't you,' and climbed into the boat. Fathers and brothers, including Dominic, pushed it from the clinging embrace of the coral sand, and the women sang softly. A slender thing of grace in its own element, the canoe moved away as the boys paddled across the pearled waters of the lagoon.

Everyone stood watching until it had negotiated the gap in the reef opposite the village, tranquil now in the slack period between the tides, but a real danger to an inexperienced sailor at any other time. The sun beat down on dark heads and serious faces as they watched the craft set off towards the horizon.

After that, solemnity forgotten, they turned away to make their talkative way back to the village. Fenella walked back with Dominic across the soft white sand to the house, feeling a strange little cold shiver.

It was still there, that faint thread of unease, when she began to get ready for her evening at the Opera House two days later. She had only one outfit that was suitable, especially as Dominic had mentioned, apparently in passing, that most people on the island enjoyed dressing up for the infrequent occasions when the Opera House was in use.

But when she had donned the sleeveless white vest she had worn the first night at Maxwell's Reach, and part-nered it with a full flowing skirt that fell to her ankles, she made a little face. It looked—well, as though she had bought a top and a skirt for their usefulness to-gether and apart. Which, of course, was exactly what she had done. In spite of her weakness for well-cut, well-made clothes, she couldn't afford to buy any that weren't going to earn their place in her wardrobe.

It meant that she missed out on the cheerful one-season trends from the chain stores, and that she wore her clothes for years, but at least, she thought, eyeing her slender form, they looked good on her. Although—did that vest show just a little too much smooth olive skin, darkened now by judicious sunbathing?

Don't be paranoid! she scoffed, but to fill in that hint of cleavage she donned a pendant that had been Paul's last present to her, a magnificent dragon in the act of flying, clutching a sapphire in its claw the exact dark blue of her eyes. Made of sterling silver, it was set with diamonds on the tips of the wing ribs, and neither the small size or the delicacy of the work could hide the feral ferocity of the beast.

Elaborate, brilliantly executed, it turned the restrained outfit into a showcase for its exquisite beauty, just as the white burnished her skin into gleaming soft gold. Brushing her black hair until it gleamed as blue as the sapphire, she left her hair down. The final touches were her silver sandals and a small white evening bag of kid.

And she hoped she looked good. Just once, she thought as she switched the light off, just once she would like to wear something outrageous and stunningly beautiful. But she had nothing that was suitable, and she wouldn't be able to afford anything that might force Dominic to look at her with—well, respect.

He was waiting in the lanai with his grandfather, leaning relaxed and graceful against the archway. Fenella's breath stopped in her lungs as she took in the superb tropical evening dress, the white dinner jacket that clung lovingly to his magnificent torso, the cummerbund and the sleek black trousers. Her heart performed an alarming somersault in her chest, and even when it had settled down it beat far more rapidly than before. She realised again that she should have said no to this outing, however much she had wanted to go.

Going out with Dominic was putting her hard-won poise in extreme jeopardy.

'Well, enjoy yourselves,' James said acerbically. 'Although why anyone would want to listen to a woman screeching——'

'Don't you dare refer to one of New Zealand's most famous opera stars as a screecher!' Fenella was laughing, for she had seen the lurking amusement in his eyes. 'She's the best soprano in the world.'

'Don't let any Australian hear you say that!'

He enjoyed playing the eternal game, the constant, mostly amiable, war of comparisons between their countries, and she had soon discovered that the only way to deal with him was to stand up to him.

'Thought that would get your goat,' he continued smugly. 'Only things New Zealand can produce, opera singers and good rugby players.' He grinned as she shook her fist at him. 'Go on, off you go and have a good time.'

But all thought of him disappeared as she accompanied Dominic out to an opulent Range Rover instead of the helicopter.

'As you've seen nothing of the island I thought we'd go the long way to Fala'isi,' he said, opening the door for her.

He probably remembered that she was inclined to get in a tizz whenever she set foot in a helicopter, she thought dismally.

However, he said nothing about that. As he set the car in motion he observed conversationally, 'Mark seems to be enjoying himself, if Pihaia is to be believed.'

Her eyes softened. 'Yes. It was a wonderful idea to call them by radio last night. Thank you.'

He slanted her a quick grin. 'I must confess I was glad to hear that they'd managed to paddle that far. Every year Pihaia is convinced that the young ones are too weak and effete to make it to the island. He always seems astonished when they prove him wrong.'

'I think he's a cunning old man,' she said. 'I'll bet his suspicions, dragged up at every available opportunity, urge each year's intake to do their best to prove him wrong!'

He chuckled, the sound smooth and intimate in the confines of the vehicle. 'Yes. I had to promise not to contact them again. He thinks it might destroy some of the *mana* of the occasion if the boys know they're in actual contact with the mainland.'

'He might be right,' she said thoughtfully. 'As it is, they can enjoy the Robinson Crusoe feeling without any of the dangers.'

'You said that rather wistfully. Would you like a desert island holiday?'

'No, but when I was Mark's age I'd have given my eye teeth to go camping.' She shrugged. 'Instead I used to spend my holidays trying not to get in people's way.'

'No camps for you?'

Shrugging, she turned her profile away from those too-shrewd eyes. 'Yes, some. I went pony-trekking once; that was fun. And I did some sailing trips. Once I went to Tahiti on a school trip to polish up my French. But when I was younger there weren't the opportunities there are now.'

Too late she realised that all these excursions had been paid for by his mother's money, channelled through his father. She waited for him to point this out, but he said nothing, and after a few seconds she relaxed, able to notice that they had pulled away from the coast and were beginning to climb through plantations of arrowroot and oranges, breadfruit and banana palms.

She commented, 'I'm surprised the road doesn't go all the way around the island.'

'The eastern side of the island is where the mountains come down to the sea; it's too rugged to have many people living there, so a road is not necessary. When Grandfather came here thirty years ago there was nothing but a foot track to Avanui.' He changed gear expertly, and avoided an alarmed chicken. It was still light, but the sun was beginning to sink into a sky the colour of rubies, deep and bright and glowing. 'He negotiated for Maxwell's Reach, and part of the price was to form and maintain an all-weather road to the village.'

She nodded. 'Clever of them.'

'Yes, wasn't it? As well, the land is on a long-term lease, with the rent negotiable every five years. The islanders are very astute, too astute to allow what has happened in so many other Pacific islands, the wholesale removal of land ownership from the indigenous people.'

'It really does sound like Paradise,' she murmured dreamily, watching the jungle come up to the edge of the road, tall and thick, looking out for the plant that bore the beautiful *tiare aloka*. Fugitive colour flamed in her cheeks. She hated to think of the villagers gossiping about whether she and Dominic were sharing a bed, but at least she didn't have to look at any of them and see knowing smiles.

Were the villagers right? Did Dominic want her as much as she wanted him? No, she thought hurriedly, keeping her eyes averted from the play of muscles in his thigh as he changed gear, of course he didn't. He despised her.

They were climbing quite steeply over the spur of some old lava flow; ahead a waterfall spilled in a veil of milk down a fearsome crag, billowing into a haze at the base before disappearing into the virid jungle. The air was cooler than on the coast, spice-scented, without the tang of the sea.

'They used to grow sugar-cane on the floor of these valleys,' he told her as they came out on to a cleared hillside above the valley. 'That was until the bottom fell out of the world sugar market, in the thirties, I think. Some is still grown, but it's only for local use. Now the land is cropped with paw-paw and mangoes and passion-fruit for the New Zealand market, as well as taro and arrowroot.'

She nodded, looking at his hands on the wheel. Lean and long-fingered, they were surprisingly deft for so big a man.

Dragging her eyes away she observed, 'No one seems to live here.'

'No, they live on the coast, so they can fish. Each village owns the land behind it and they commute to their gardens on horses or motorbikes or little jeep affairs. The system works well.'

They were swooping down towards the valley when a pig ran squealing across the road. Fenella gasped, but Dominic's reflexes were excellent. He took them to the edge of the cliff, but managed to keep them on the road and miss the demented animal, now charging noisily up through the bush.

'Sorry,' he said with a brief glance at her. 'All right?'

'Yes. Yes, I'm fine, thank you.'

'They're a natural hazard, one of the reasons why no one drives very fast.'

Once down on the valley floor they travelled beside a little brook that turned into a deep tidal stream, darkly mysterious beneath large trees in the gathering twilight. The road joined another wider one and headed on around the coast, offering glimpses of the sea through ironwoods and the ubiquitous coconut palms.

They passed through small settlements where people rode cheerfully along the road, smiling and waving to them with a pleasure that made it obvious they recognised the Range Rover. Frangipani bushes bloomed in a multitude of colours from white through cream and gold and pink to various shades of pink and a magnificent deep rose. Neat houses were set in villages, each one exquisitely tidy, all surrounded by plantations leading up into the foothills.

And then they were in Fala'isi, the little town with its port and airport and hotels.

'What causes the gaps through the reef?' asked Fenella, remembering how she had seen one opposite the little town from the plane as they came in to land.

'Rivers. Coral can't grow in fresh or even brackish water, so wherever a river or largeish stream comes down from the mountains there's a break in the reef. Fala'isi is built on the biggest river on the island, which means its pass is the biggest. The harbour is the reason why the town was built there.'

'I see.' She leaned forward as they came into the town centre, alive and active as any tourist town, but with a large number of the locals sauntering along the footpaths, clearly as interested in the tourists as the tourists were in them.

'Here we are.' The vehicle slid into a parking area, to be met by a large man in uniform. As he opened Fenella's door the attendant beamed cheerfully and asked Dominic how his grandfather was.

'He's improving, thank you.' Dominic handed over his keys.

'Ah, you can't keep that old man down. You tell him Rata was asking about him.'

'I'll do that. He sends his regards, by the way.'

Rata's grin widened even further. 'You going to the concert?'

'Yes.'

'Rather you than me, man. I'll be waiting for you round about ten-thirty, then.'

'Thank you.' Dominic took Fenella's arm. 'The restaurant is only a few yards up the road, and the Opera House only a few more yards further on.'

The restaurant opened from a narrow door into a series of rooms, some separated by full walls, others by thick greenery, so that it looked like a pavilion in a forest.

Fenella was looking around with frank interest when a head waiter in immaculate evening dress came gliding towards them. He didn't ask their names, merely exchanged a brief smile with Dominic and murmured, 'Good evening,' to Fenella as he escorted them through the room to a table set well out of the way, separated from the rest by a long trough of graceful bamboo that reached almost to the ceiling.

From his appearance she guessed that the food was to be Oriental, but she would never have guessed it from the decorations, which were severely modern.

After seating them the head waiter looked up and another waiter appeared with the menus. He moved just as silently, was just as unobtrusive as the head waiter had been.

Fenella looked at the menu with a dismay she hoped was concealed. None of the names were familiar to her; in most cases she had no idea what they were, and there were no little explanations printed beside the exotic-sounding dishes.

'How do you like your food?' asked Dominic. 'Hot, super-hot or solar temperature?'

She chuckled. 'Just hot. And what would you have done if I'd said I didn't like hot food?'

'Told them to cool it down, and tried not to hear the cooks cry,' he said, his mouth curving in a smile that made her toes curl in the pretty silver sandals. 'Don't worry, they're used to cowards. Now, do you trust me to order?'

'Yes.' It was odd, but she did.

He looked up, and instantly the waiter materialised. From the way Dominic pronounced the exotic names she wondered whether he spoke whatever language this was too, although they conferred together in English.

As soon as the food had been ordered another man came up with a wine list. Dominic looked at it casually, ordered a Sauvignon Blanc from New Zealand's Marlborough, in the South Island, and said with a quirking smile, 'Just so you don't feel so far away from home.'

The meal was delicious. Fenella thought she had never eaten anything so superb in all her life as the delicacies that were put in front of her, none of them, to her surprise, too hot, although most had been prepared with chili. She recognised crab, and the flavour of lemon grass, and a delicious satay, but the spicy aromas and subtle, intriguing tastes were entirely new to her. When at last

she put down the chopsticks and sighed in delicate re-
pletion she still didn't know whether this was Chinese
cooking or from some other Oriental country; she just
knew that it was an art form in itself.

'Is it what you expected?' Dominic asked, his voice
amused.

She permitted herself a sardonic smile. 'Chicken chow
mein and chop suey? Hardly. Is it Chinese cooking?'

'No—Thai. It's not particularly well known and many
people find it too hot, but I like it.'

'As of now,' she said devoutly, 'so do I.'

She knew her expression revealed just how much she
was enjoying herself, but was incapable of controlling
it. Halfway through the meal she had found herself
wondering whether this was the man who thought her
little better than a slut, who considered her mother no
more than that, the same Dominic Maxwell who had
warned her that her relationship to Mark would gain her
no entry to the circles he moved in.

Now she understood why so many women were only
too eager to put up with the stringent constraints he insisted on in his social life. He was fascinating, the green
eyes glittering with sparks of awareness whenever he
looked at her, his formidable attention bent only on her.
They might have been the only two people in the world,
and from the way he looked at her she could have been
the only woman who had ever interested him. It had to
be a technique he had refined over many such evenings,
but alas, she was all too susceptible to it.

It was in a state of dazzled exaltation that she refused
another course. Coffee, she thought with possibly her
last remnant of common sense, would bring her down
from these realms of fantasy, sober her up.

However, the coffee, although delicious and strong,
did nothing to disperse the fumes in her brain. Still as
potently aware of his masculine worldliness, she walked
silently beside him in a soft scented air towards the en-
chanting little Opera House, elegantly Victorian on its

hill below the other relic of the days of the Empire, the small cathedral.

Others were walking too, the women dressed in their best, men in evening dress. Dominic was content to respect her silence, nor did he touch her except when she tripped on a crack in the footpath. Then his hand caught her elbow so quickly that she had time to do little more than stagger. A current of electricity ran from his fingers to her most secret places, and she was glad when he murmured, 'All right?' and, at her nod, dropped his hand.

They strolled on beneath the huge silk cotton trees planted in the square to shade the passers-by. From their large pods the last of the kapok floss that gave them their name was drifting on the gentle breeze to pile up in creamy mounds of cotton wool in the corners and against railings.

Fenella drew deeply of the frangipani-scented breeze. She could, she thought foolishly, ask for nothing more than this in all her life, just to walk with Dominic Maxwell through a tropical night, full of delicious food, on the way to hear one of the world's greatest sopranos.

The evening was better than any dream, any fantasy. The opera star sang exquisitely, her beautiful voice casting a spell over the eager audience, and gave them the four encores they demanded.

When it was over Fenella sighed, her lashes resting for a second on her cheeks as she tried to regain some control. She felt dangerously disorientated, snatched from her normal life into the middle of a fairytale, and she thought, with a fleeting glance at the boldly handsome features of the man beside her, that if she had any sense at all she would jerk herself free of the lingering enchantment he seemed to have enmeshed her in and run like a terrified antelope all the way back to New Zealand.

But just for tonight, her heart whispered. What harm can come to you just for the night?

This time he took her arm, protecting her from the jostle of patrons as they came out on to the footpath. Dominic nodded to several people, but something in his mien discouraged any further approaches. Fenella felt the impact of many curious, speculative glances.

She didn't care. In fact, she revelled in the knowledge that it was she who was with him, that the envy in those feminine eyes was directed at her, that other women wished they were with the man who towered over most of the others, severe and overwhelmingly masculine in his evening clothes.

The soft material of her skirt about her, the warm weight of the dragon on her breast, its stones winking in the lights, the hazy caress of the air—all seemed heightened, intensified by the lingering aftermath of the rapturously romantic music and the magic of the night and her response to the man beside her.

Dominic's fingers were firm on her bare arm, and his faint, essentially mysterious, masculine scent blended with the fragrance of the Pacific night, striking beneath her common sense to appeal directly to primitive needs buried deep within her.

A few paces in front of them a slender blonde woman with a sweet, beautiful face looked over her shoulder and saw Dominic. Instantly her face lit up into the sort of smile that probably made ancient Troy's walls crumble. The man with her, a tall lean sophisticate with an arrogant pirate's countenance that hinted at a Mediterranean ancestry, looked back too, and a smile softened the hard lines of his face.

Risking a quick upwards glance, Fenella saw Dominic's sculpted mouth pull in slightly at the corners, and wondered why he didn't like the newcomers, whoever they were.

But when he greeted them it was without the slightest stiffness. 'Tamsyn,' he said, with a blatantly appreciative smile as he bent to kiss the woman's cheek. 'And Grant. I should have expected to see you, of course.

Tamsyn is a New Zealander like you, Fenella. Naturally you'd come to hear your favourite singer.'

And with that he introduced her to the Chapmans, who were, she gathered, important people on Fala'isi. And in other parts of the world as well, she decided, reacting to the innate authority that Grant Chapman shared with the man beside her.

Fenella was slightly intimidated by their sophisticated gloss, but they were so pleasant that she wasn't allowed to be shy, and within a few seconds she had relaxed, taking her part in the conversation with an ease that astounded her.

Tamsyn Chapman said, 'We're having a small party at the plantation after this, just a few drinks. If I'd known you were here, Dominic, I'd have asked you both, of course. Why don't you come along?'

Very smoothly he answered, 'We'd enjoy that very much, but if you don't mind I want to get back home. I don't like leaving Grandfather for too long.'

Now what had he said that brought that glimmer of amusement to Grant Chapman's striking face? It was gone in an instant, but Fenella's uneasiness returned at full flood.

She stood quietly as Tamsyn Chapman said sympathetically, 'Of course you must go, I should have thought of that. But we must get together, all of us, soon.' She bestowed that lovely smile on Fenella. 'It's a year or so since I was in Auckland, so I'd love to hear what's happening there.'

Dominic's excuse was a reasonable one; he was a good grandson who unobtrusively put his grandfather first, yet he knew, even if the Chapmans didn't, that James Maxwell had his nurse with him.

So why had he refused the invitation? As they walked back to the car, Fenella found herself wondering with a sick bleakness whether perhaps Dominic was ashamed of her.

CHAPTER SIX

ALL THROUGH the quiet discussion on the way home, of the merits of the singer, her choice of arias and the delights of the ravishing little Opera House, the humiliating doubts ate into Fenella.

It had been impossible to tell what Dominic was thinking as he introduced her; he controlled his expression too well, revealing only what he wanted of his thoughts. But he certainly hadn't seemed ashamed of her in the restaurant.

Although, the voice niggling at the back of her brain reminded her, they might as well have been alone at the restaurant. He had reserved a table that was separated from the rest of the room, unable to be overlooked. At the time she had thought it was because he, like her, wanted the illusion of being alone together.

Were her clothes not up to par? She looked down at the white fabric flowing over her thighs. Tamsyn Chapman's dress had been absolutely magnificent, sleek and restrained and sophisticated, the creation of some great designer, but it had not suited her blonde beauty any more than this outfit suited Fenella.

Not given to false modesty, she knew that the white vest and skirt made the most of her high bust and narrow waist and called attention to her long legs and slender feet. And although the dragon resting comfortably in the sleek satin hollow above the rise of her breasts could not be compared to the superb string of pearls about the other woman's throat, it was no cheap, badly made piece of jewellery.

What did it matter that her clothes didn't have a Parisian couturier's label? They were cut cleverly and well made.

'Stop it!' she adjured herself fiercely beneath her breath, well aware of what she was doing to herself.

'I'm sorry, I didn't hear you.'

Appalled, she watched her hands clench in her lap. 'Nothing,' she muttered, miserably aware of her vulnerability where this man was concerned.

Dominic asked, 'Did you want to go to Tamsyn's party? I'm sorry, I should have realised——'

Some note in the deep voice made her wince. She broke in, 'No, not at all. I'm not sulking.'

He sounded amused. 'I didn't accuse you of that.'

'Oh, well, if I'd been sitting here brooding about it, that would have been pretty close to a monster sulk, don't you think?' She couldn't prevent the snap in her voice.

'And that's not your style?'

'No,' she said, quietly now. 'I despise people who sulk—it's such a petty reaction. I prefer to blow up and get it out of my system.'

'Then why don't you tell me what's upset you?' he suggested calmly. 'You were enjoying yourself during dinner, and the concert, but since we met the Chapmans you've subsided into silence. And sulking apart, I don't think it's a contented silence. It seems more like brooding, that ominous stillness before a volcano blows.'

His perception so unnerved her that she returned baldly, 'I wondered why you didn't want to go to the Chapmans' house. I thought perhaps it was because you consider I'm not good enough for your friends.'

There was a frozen silence. She drew a deep breath and blurted out, 'Of course, if it's simply that you're carrying out the threat you made when I first arrived, to make sure I didn't enjoy any social life—well, that's fair enough. But if that's so, I don't know why you asked me out.'

His hands tightened on the wheel. Abruptly he wrenched it, pulling the vehicle on to the side of the road. The engine died. Fenella swallowed, wondering stupidly why she hadn't just kept her mouth shut. In the sudden silence and darkness his burnished voice was infinitely more intimidating than open rage would have been.

'If I hadn't wanted you with me I wouldn't have suggested you come. When I saw you tonight I thought you looked like every man's dream, long and elegant and silky with your golden skin and your soft red mouth. And as well as looking like a dream you can discuss the pros and cons of the Green movement without getting fanatical, you have a sly sense of humour, your table manners are exquisite. What in the name of God is there to be ashamed of? I know I should have asked you whether you wanted to go on, at least by implication, but I'm accustomed to making decisions alone, and this one I felt strongly about. Didn't you see Grant smile? He knew damned well that I wanted to be alone with you.'

Sudden wonder held her silent for just too long. Dominic gave a savage laugh and leaned over, pulling her face around so that he could kiss her with a slow experienced passion that made her heart soar.

When it was over he lifted his mouth a fraction of an inch from hers and said on an expelled breath, 'Don't ever make that mistake again. What you are is infinitely more important than who you are. You may well have been lumbered with a poisonous pair for parents, but you haven't got that on your own. My own,' he finished grimly, 'are no great example.'

Something, some note of—knowledge—in his voice made her whisper, 'You know who my father is, don't you?'

He didn't have to say anything; she read it in the sudden stillness of his big body. But he said slowly, as though testing her, 'Yes, I do.'

'I see.' She blinked, pulling away a fraction.

Dominic swore, released her and said curtly, 'This is no place to be discussing things. Wait until we get home.'

They drove the rest of the way in silence, Fenella staring with unseeing eyes through the windscreen as the thoughts whirled wildly around her head.

It seemed bitterly ironic to her that everyone else seemed to know all about her; that she, the one who was most affected, knew the least.

Was her father still alive? Did she have relatives, perhaps half-sisters or brothers, and if so, did she want to contact them?

And what did that kiss mean? That he wanted her? Or was it just his way of proving that he was not ashamed of her?

Back at Maxwell's Reach she allowed Dominic to take her arm and escort her into the big sitting-room with its cream sofas and coffee-tables, the smooth cream marble of their tops contrasting with the classically wrought iron legs. Dominic switched on a lamp the same colour as the marble and the fabric of the upholstery, and turned to scan her face keenly, no emotion in the pale depths of his eyes.

Mutely she returned his survey, her expression held firmly under control.

He said evenly, 'He's dead now, he died about fourteen years ago. He was a doctor in Dunedin, with a wife but no children. Your mother became his lover just after she turned eighteen, when he was in his mid-thirties.'

'Eighteen?' The word trembled with shock and horror.

His face hardened. 'Yes. He should have been shot. However, I'm sure you remember how beautiful she was; at eighteen she must have been breathtaking. Well, I know she was; I have only to remember what you were like when you were sixteen. I don't think the poor devil stood a chance.'

Fenella bit her lip to stop them from trembling. 'Why didn't he divorce his wife?' she asked.

The massive shoulders moved in a slight shrug. 'His wife was a sophisticated woman, a good hostess with excellent connections who suited him down to the ground. I imagine he never intended to break up his marriage.'

'So my mother was—a bit on the side,' she supplied in a dead little voice.

Dominic nodded, watching her keenly, although there was no warmth in his gaze. 'I'm afraid so. He set her up in a flat, and visited her whenever he could.'

Closing her eyes, Fenella realised now why he had been so ready to believe the worst of her mother. Nausea made clammy beads of sweat spring out along her top lip. She fought it down ruthlessly. 'I must have come as a shock to him,' she said without expression.

Again the slight shrug. 'To him, yes. Not to her, I gather.'

The scenario this suggested made her wince. 'Was I to be the means of forcing him to leave his wife?'

'It seems logical,' he said, choosing his words carefully, yet making no attempt to soften the blow. 'She did, after all, try the same stunt with my father.'

Fenella nodded, turning her head away so that he couldn't see the stark anguish on her face. She recalled how, home from school, she had been reading in her bedroom when her mother had told Simon that she was pregnant. It was the only time that she saw him angry with her mother.

A painful smile twisted her mouth. The reason the recollection was so clear was that in the ensuing altercation he had said that one child was too many, and the words had been seared into her mind.

'So you were right when you said she had only a few tricks. Poor Mum,' she said softly, groping for some sort of composure, 'you were right, she didn't have much imagination, did she? No wonder she never liked me much! Although she adored Mark.'

He reached out and caught her up, pulling her close into the warmth and support of his big body, his arms wonderfully gentle about her. 'You didn't have much of a childhood, did you? A pawn for essentially selfish people... But if it's any consolation, when your father wanted your mother to have an abortion, she refused. Instead she packed up and left Dunedin.'

'She probably hoped I'd be a boy so that she could use him to extract money from his father,' she said stonily.

He swore beneath his breath, but his hands were wonderfully gentle on her body. 'He paid maintenance for you until the day he died,' he said.

The harshness of his tone made her think him uncaring, but when she looked up, wincing, she saw concern and a deep self-directed anger in his expression. Or perhaps he was still angry with her mother, the woman he thought she resembled. Oh, he was being wonderfully kind, but that meant nothing. He was sorry he had hurt her, but he would tell her no lies. Yet his brutal honesty was oddly cleansing, after the falseness she had lived with all her life.

Shame made her lower her lashes.

'We won't ever know why she did the things she did,' he said, kissing her cold forehead, warming her with his vitality. 'But none of what happened had anything to do with you. I'm sorry you had to hear it like this.'

Fenella shivered. The temptation to give in to the pain and anger and straight outrage that was tearing her in two was almost irresistible. If she relaxed in his arms and let him hold her, he would enfold her in the protectiveness that she was beginning to see was the other side of his great strength.

And she wanted to let him, she needed his warmth, his vitality, something to hold back the cold...

But in the end she would be alone again, encumbered by emotions she couldn't face, hadn't learned to deal with.

So she eased herself out of his debilitating embrace, her face as smooth and expressionless as a mask. 'I think I'll go to bed now,' she said without emotion. 'Thank you—I enjoyed the evening very much.'

Dominic's mouth curled in a sardonic little smile, but he let her go without saying a word, although she felt his watchful gaze all the way to the door. In a way she was grateful for his calm, unsparing attitude. If he had

offered her any sympathy beyond the muteness of
contact, she would have broken down and bawled like
a child in front of him. At least this way she had sal-
vaged some dignity.

Soundlessly she walked down the long arcaded
passage. The lovely bedroom that had always seemed to
view her as an intruding presence now seemed like a
sanctuary. Keeping her mind away from Dominic's revelations, she showered and cleaned the cosmetics from
her face, then without thinking pulled on the white satin
robe she had never used because she was terrified of
marking the fabric.

Absently she set the silver piping straight down her
lap as she curled up in the white armchair. From the
darkened bedroom she could see out past the terrace to
beyond the pool and the jagged silhouettes of the mountains, for once free of mist, although a high bank of thin
cloud fuzzed the stars above them.

Only then, with the little frogs calling from the grass
and the trees, did she allow herself to think about what
Dominic had told her.

It explained a lot, she thought, her hand sliding up
and down the soft shining material in an aimless little
movement over her knee.

But there was much that no one would ever know.
Whether her mother had truly loved her father, for one.
It didn't seem as though he had loved her.

No wonder she had been so distant; it would have been
difficult to love a child whose father had seduced her
and then betrayed her. Tears filled Fenella's eyes. She
wiped them with the back of her hand and let her head
fall back to rest on the back of the chair. Her breasts
rose and fell as she drew a deep, shuddering breath.

So now she knew why Dominic had been so convinced
that her mother wanted security so much that she had
insisted on that bigamous marriage. Perhaps, Fenella
thought in sick anguish, it also explained why he had
kissed her mother's sixteen-year-old daughter with such
unbridled hunger. After all, she had been only two years

younger than her mother had been when she first slept with her father.

But no, even as the thought formulated, she knew that it was wrong. That kiss had been rage expressed in sexuality. It had meant nothing beyond the fact that he was furious with her, and because he wasn't the sort of brute who hit women he had kissed her.

At least that was how it had begun, but in the end it had become more than the straight impulse to dominate a defiant woman with the strength of his masculinity. If he knew that it had been seared into her memory all these years, that because of it she had never been able to give herself to any other man, he would probably be shocked.

If it was possible to shock him, which she doubted. Horrified, more like.

She smiled bleakly into the darkness, her eyes fixed on the white glimmer of the orchids. Now she knew why they were called moth orchids. That was exactly what they looked like, exquisite white moths resting a moment in her room. Her mind flew back to the *tiare aloka*, the crimson stars of the flower of love, and this time she couldn't stop the tears. They knotted in her throat, then burst free. Surrendering to them, Fenella buried her face in her hands, uncaring of the pristine white robe or the romance of the tropical night outside, weeping for everything that had gone so wrong.

He came so silently that her first knowledge of his presence was his hands on her shoulders, pulling her up as effortlessly as though she were a baby and then lifting her, cradling her to him when he sat down in the chair and held her on his lap, turning her face to sob into his neck while his hand moved slowly, comfortingly over her back.

She wept without restraint, using the handkerchief he gave her, aware even through her tears of the fact that it bore his own essential scent.

'I'm sorry,' she hiccuped at last.

He made no reply, but that wonderfully soothing hand went to the tangled mass of her hair and began threading through it as though it were the finest silk in a caress so gentle that she felt fresh tears well up.

'Don't be so nice,' she muttered soggily. 'It'll only make me bawl more.'

'So?' His voice was harsh. 'Crying is good for the soul, I believe.'

She blew her nose and gave in to temptation, leaning her cheek against his chest, resting dreamily against his hardness, surrendering to his strength with shameless abandon. He was warm and hard, like a living rock, and the size which had seemed so intimidating at first now seemed just right.

'I'm sorry,' she sighed again.

'I take it you don't very often cry.'

She said in some surprise, 'I can't remember the last time I did.'

'So you bottle it all up.'

'Well—perhaps.'

'That's supposed to be extremely bad for you.'

She laughed a little. 'Do you cry?'

'Not a lot,' he said drily. 'But I have.'

He must have sensed her astonishment, for she felt laughter lift the wall of his chest. 'Did you think I was made of granite?'

'If I did it's because that's the impression you tried very hard to put across. For most of the times we've seen each other, anyway.'

'Astute woman!' The tone was teasing, but she realised it would be useless to ask him why.

So she let her cheek rest against the comforting thud of his heartbeats and gave herself up to feeling cherished and protected. Of course he hadn't changed his mind about her; no doubt he still thought she was an adventuress on the make. And the wild sensual attraction was still there; it was just momentarily submerged by this sweet moment of communion, into which she should read nothing more than his regret that she should learn about her parents' affair from him.

As well as hard and authoritative, Dominic was a decent man, she decided. Not kind, or particularly gentle, but he had the right instincts.

Caveman instincts; he took what he wanted, but he protected those weaker than himself. Or at least the women and children. He had been generous with his time and attention to Mark, and there was no doubt that he loved his grandfather. And in his own ruthlessly honest way he had been kind to her, too.

Sighing, Fenella turned her head into his throat and slid her hands under his arms. The fingers slipping through her hair paused a moment, then resumed, separating out the strands of warm silk as though their feel was pleasant to him.

She could have purred. The gentle sensuous movements sent shivers of response all the way through her, small increments of heat that started in her skin and lapped slowly, inevitably along every nerve, into every cell.

The quality of his caress, and of her reaction, changed between one heartbeat and the next. Outside the little frogs called, summoning a mate in the only way they knew. In the quiet room the signals were infinitely more subtle but just as compelling. Fenella's arms tightened about Dominic's broad chest; the hand in her hair clenched a little, urging her head back. In answer she lifted her face, her eyes dilating so that the colour, blue as the midnight outside, was nothing more than a rim around the dilated pupils.

Bronzed skin drawn taut over the starkly brutal contours of his features, he stared at her for long moments, his eyes crystalline yet lit by flames as intense as the Southern Lights in the green of an Antarctic sky, his mouth a hard straight line that was disturbingly insistent.

Fenella heard the beat of her heart mingle with the sound of his, the two disparate rhythms blending to make a muted thunder. So strong that she could taste it, that it filled her nostrils, desire broke through her like the outburst of a nova.

He made a soft, guttural noise in his throat, barely audible, yet she knew it for what it was, the final relinquishment of control. As his mouth came down to claim hers her lashes fluttered shut.

There were no preliminaries, no gentle teasing, no soft caresses. He broke through her defences with all the power of a tropical cyclone, storming her mouth and carrying all before him, mastering her completely with one kiss, one deep exploration.

Yet there was no cruelty in it, no hidden agenda. His desire was as untrammelled as the night, open, frank, a force of nature that matched and met hers, demanding a like response, an equal passion.

Linking her arms around his neck, Fenella pulled herself up a little, and the kiss eased, but before she had time to slide her hand beneath his shirt his mouth took hers again, as though he couldn't bear to leave it, as though she was some kind of obsession to him, a necessity as vital as air and fire, as the cool caress of the water and the warm heat of the sun.

Any memory of the kisses she had experienced previously, even his, faded and died, buried in the hot reality of this. She strained upwards, exploring as deeply, searching, taking, making herself cognisant of his rapacious mouth in a partnership as old as time. Racked by rigours, her body arched. Sensation burst inside her in a blind primeval surge, demanding satisfaction, completion, demanding something she had never experienced because, she realised dimly, only this man, only Dominic could give it to her.

In the sudden involuntary hardening of his body she recognised a savage hunger that surrounded her with a miasma of carnality. She twisted, her hips moving in a way as old as time, her arms tightening around the heat and strength of his shoulders, lost in a desire more potent than anything she had ever felt.

'Not so fast,' he said softly, his beautiful voice rough with emotion. 'Let me see...'

His hand slid beneath the white satin, pulling the lapels apart to reveal her breasts, pale globes against the white of the robe, its satin not any more smooth, any more soft than they.

A dark fire blazed in his eyes. As Fenella followed his eyes down a strange drawing collected in the crumpled dusky tips, and to her astonishment she saw them stand proudly forth. She gave a low cry, aching for an unknown fulfilment. His arms contracted around her and he lifted her until he could take her breast in his mouth.

Another sound was wrenched from her. Liquid fire burned deep in the pit of her stomach as a spear of sensation ran through her from his suckling mouth to the junction of her thighs.

Moaning, she held his head against her, her fingers clutching the thick dark hair, lost in an enchantment of need and desire. He turned her slightly so that he could claim the other breast, make it his with the fire of his caress, and then he kissed her mouth again, and her throat, and the hollow at its base, the soft mounds of her breasts, his mouth closing with a little more force than before, slightly marking the satin skin with the heat of his hunger.

Clutching, desperate, all caution washed away in an agony of need, Fenella groaned his name. His thumb over her nipple sent shafts of exquisite agony streaking through her as he said deeply, roughly, 'If we don't call a halt now, Fenella, I'm going to take you across to your bed and bury myself deep in that satin body of yours and not leave you or your bed until I'm sated.'

The words were unbearably stimulating, but even as she thrilled to them cold sanity was banishing the clouds from her brain. Only a few minutes before she had had to face what passion could do to people, the mess it could make of their lives.

She said in a shaking voice, 'There's nothing more I'd like than for you to do that, but I—no.'

Resting his brow against her breasts, Dominic turned it so that the rough satin of his cheeks stimulated them into new, feverish life.

'Sensible,' he muttered in a strained voice. 'I've always hated that word. But you're right—it would confuse too many issues.'

Already she wanted to repeal her decision, throw caution and sense and wisdom, all the sober workaday virtues, out through the window and follow the voyagers who had lost their hearts to the South Seas down the path of their desires. But she was too afraid. If she made love with him, she would be putting not only her heart but her future in jeopardy.

So she summoned what was left of her resolution and leaned her head on his, hoping he would not know just how much her decision had cost her. They sat there for some moments in silent communion while the humming intensity of the sexuality they had awakened faded into some sort of controllable emotion.

At last Dominic lifted his head and looked for a long time at the softness that had cushioned his cheek. As he pulled the lapels of the robe together he said quietly, 'You have skin like the pearls from one particular atoll in the Pacific. They have a golden sheen that's mysterious and powerfully appealing, but so few women have the colouring to wear them that they're not worth farming.'

He smiled ironically at the colour that warmed not only her cheeks but her breasts. 'They have all the allure of the Pacific, the warmth and the sensuous smoothness, and the danger, because they're fished the old way, by men who dive to the bottom of the lagoon and put their lives on the line. Ah, you don't like the thought of that?'

'No,' she said quietly, getting to her feet, suddenly cold without his arms around her. Flicking the mass of sable hair back from her face, she moved away from the armchair, eager to put some distance between herself and the potent lure of his masculinity. 'I don't think I could wear pearls that had caused pain or death.'

His mouth twisted cynically as he got up, latent power in the lithe movement. 'Some women find that adds to the appeal.'

'Not me.' He was too big, too close. Fenella moved a little further away, her lashes falling to hide the confusion that racked her.

'No, I can see that.' He was watching her, his eyes almost closed, although in the starlit room she could see the narrow glint of green beneath those long lashes.

Nervously she clutched the robe across her breasts, moved back with long-legged grace, her skin pulling tight as she reacted helplessly to his heavy-lidded survey.

'I'll see you in the morning,' he said after a moment. She nodded, desperate for him to be gone.

But he said, 'Don't go wallowing in remorse or shame, Fenella. What happened tonight was as sweet as anything I've ever experienced, and we both know that it's been inevitable since—well, since you came to Fala'isi. Goodnight.'

'Goodnight,' she replied, her voice high-pitched and nervous.

She managed to get to sleep, although it took her a long time, lying still in the big bed, learning to resent the shrill calls of the little frogs while in the background the big Pacific combers rolled in from thousands of miles of ocean to smash themselves on to the remorseless reef.

Naturally she woke late in the morning. The tea-tray was still beside the bed, but the tea was long cold. She waited until she thought that with any luck Dominic had gone out, either fishing as he did periodically, or sailing— somewhere where she didn't have to face him for a while.

Then she showered and dressed in a sober shirtwaister that was just a little hot for the unpleasant temperature; it was much stickier and hotter than it had been since they arrived on the island. Hiding a certain amount of embarrassment, she strolled along the terrace.

James was not in evidence, but she came across Mari talking to Peter Brown, and smiled warmly at the self-effacing but pleasant man who fulfilled the position of nurse as well as valet to the old man.

They broke off their discussion a little abruptly.

'Is everything all right?' she asked, compelled by some uneasiness at the back of her mind.

Peter Brown gave her a pleasant smile. 'Yes, everything's fine. Mr Maxwell finds this sort of weather very trying, so he intends to spend the day in his bedroom, where it's air-conditioned.'

'Is there anything I can do for him?' she asked automatically.

He looked a bit taken aback but responded pleasantly, 'No, he's all right, thank you.' His eyes twinkled. 'I've no doubt that if he wants you he'll let you know.'

Fenella chuckled. 'Oh, I'm sure he will.'

'Ah, well I dare say you don't get to head your own big corporation if you're a retiring violet,' he said comfortably. 'I'd better go, I suppose.'

'Where's Dominic?' Fenella asked before she could stop herself.

Mari and Peter Brown exchanged looks. 'He went off to town in the Range Rover,' Peter offered as he turned to go. 'He should be back soon.'

Fenella's embarrassment was relieved by Mari's crisp question. 'Do you want something to eat?'

Fenella gave her a blank look. 'No, I don't think so. It's too hot.'

'You'd better have something or you'll feel sick.'

Fenella smiled faintly. 'All right, then, just some fruit.'

'And coffee?'

'Yes, coffee. Definitely coffee.'

Mari gave her an odd sideways grin that made her remember the housekeeper's part in arranging that wreath of *tiara aloka*. For a moment she hesitated, wondering whether she should say anything, but common sense kept her silent. Dominic and James must know that Mari discussed their sleeping arrangements with the women of the village. If they didn't mind, and clearly they didn't, why should she?

After all, nothing had happened—and nothing was going to.

For with the morning had come the counsel she should have listened to the night before, the wisdom that told her she should have nothing further to do with Dominic.

Last night's events made her shrivel with shame; what on earth had she been thinking of, for heaven's sake, to give in so wantonly to the needs and desires she had successfully repressed until then?

It was too easy to say that she had been thrown by Dominic's recital of the sordid circumstances of her conception, but that was only half the truth.

The other half, much less palatable, but which had to be faced, was that she had wanted him ever since she was sixteen, and last night it had all boiled over and if he hadn't called a halt—for of course that was what he had done—she would have woken this morning as his lover.

Even as something deep inside her melted at the thought of it, she shuddered. It would have been a disaster. She was not her mother, prepared to be a man's mistress while hoping that in time he would divorce his wife and offer her the security of marriage.

She would want Dominic with all her heart, all of him. Anything less would slowly kill some essential part of her. And although he had said that he wanted her, that he hungered for her, he hadn't said a word about love.

Fenella was slowly coming to realise that she could be content with nothing less.

The waves thundered heavily on the reef. Restlessly she wandered to the other side of the house and gazed out to sea, watching the spray as it flew high in the air.

In spite of the noise the breakers moved sluggishly, as though enervated by the stifling, suffocating heat. The lagoon was the colour of lead, flat and still in the motionless air. Not a thing moved, not a coconut frond, not a bird, not a brilliant papery flower on the bougainvillaea.

Made uneasy by a sky almost covered by a high, thin layer of cirrus cloud, she turned away and went back to the terrace, once more resuming the treadmill of thoughts and fears that had been rolling through her brain since she woke up.

She would have to make sure it didn't happen again. She was altogether too susceptible to that raw masculine appeal. Next time, she thought with an odd sinking feeling, next time she just might succumb, and then she would be set on a course with no destination but shame and pain.

Mari was a welcome interruption, arriving with toast and beautifully arranged slices of paw-paw, its glistening apricot flesh tantalising against white china. Tucked into it was an orchid, the green and vanilla shadings of the petals a delicate, exquisite contrast to the fruit.

The Islanders delighted in such beautiful trifles, and their love of flowers was legendary and everywhere apparent. The maids always had frangipani or one of the other blossoms about their persons, and she had never seen Mari without a hibiscus in her dark hair. Somehow it seemed right on her, its gaudy silken brashness not at all detrimental to her middle-aged dignity.

'The weather seems funny,' Fenella commented after thanking her. 'Are we in for a storm?'

Mari shrugged, her mobile face expressing resignation. 'In for some rain, anyway. Summer is the time we get most of it here, although it comes any time of year.'

'It seems—unusual.'

The housekeeper said shrewdly, 'You worry too much about that brother of yours. He's a good kid, sensible, not stupid, and old Pihaia didn't get to be old by taking risks. If the barometer drops too much Dominic will know what to do.'

Fenella's sober, 'Yes, I know,' astonished even herself. Like everyone else, she had succumbed to that air of masterful competence that permeated Dominic like an aura.

Last night too; even before his kisses had told her that he was far more experienced than she was, she had known that he would make love with a passionate skill that would transport her beyond herself.

Stop it!

Comforted by her instinctive trust in his ability to do anything that was necessary for Mark's safety, her inchoate fears relieved, she ate a piece of toast and demolished the fruit, drank two cups of coffee, then took the dishes into the big super-efficient kitchen and washed them up, until she was found and shooed out with much giggling by the younger of the two maids who helped Mari run the house.

It was still unbearably hot, and seemed to be getting hotter. Fenella swam in the lagoon hoping that it would be cooler than the pool, but the water was lukewarm and enervating and the air pressed heavily down on her, so she dragged herself out unrefreshed and almost hotter than when she had started.

A pointless exercise, she thought grumpily, as she showered, succumbing to the heat by donning a loose shift with no waist.

Refusing to admit that she was missing Dominic, she tried to read, but after five minutes put the book aside with an exclamation of disgust. An intolerable restlessness ached through her. Perhaps she could try to sketch the scene, capture that vaguely menacing quality of the atmosphere.

Sketchbook in hand, she wandered out to the seaward side of the house and stared frowningly out across the lagoon. Yes, the breakers were definitely higher than they had been, and the sea itself was rougher, with one or two whitecaps marring the sullen grey. A wall of water thundered down on the reef, the crest curling above the mass of solid water, then falling, white and turbulent, as the breaker shattered on the unforgiving reef. From one of the *motu* a great flock of black frigate birds flew screaming into the air, then settled back down again.

'Dominic, where are you?' she whispered, aware that she was behaving stupidly yet unable to stop herself.

Uneasily, the impulse to sketch forgotten, she went back to the house. But she couldn't settle; the lush beauty of the gardens failed to calm her, and she even wandered down to the landing pad, noting absently that the helicopter was tied very securely down in its concrete hangar.

An hour later she was definitely edgy. Even to her inexperienced eyes it was obvious that the sea was getting bigger and more threatening as the hours wore on. The measure of her nervousness was the relief with which she heard the welcome sound of a vehicle pulling up outside Maxwell's Reach.

She had almost reached the lanai when she heard his hard voice talking rapidly, an incisive note in it somehow coalescing all her vague fears into certainty. Biting her lip, she hesitated, then set her jaw and kept going.

Peter Brown was with him, his alarmed expression lending credibility to the unease that had gripped her all morning. Her eyes flew to where Dominic was standing, his long, tanned fingers turning the dial on the radio.

'What is it?' she demanded as the announcer's voice burst into the room. 'What's happening?'

CHAPTER SEVEN

WITHOUT looking up, he commanded curtly, 'Quiet!'

Fenella froze, her attention caught by an ominous few words from the radio announcer. 'What was that?' she whispered. 'What did he say?'

Dominic said calmly, 'Apparently another bloody cyclone, Peta this time, has spawned. There's going to be no bumbling around with this one. It's heading straight for us.'

A coldness gripped her. She swallowed, her eyes darkening to flat opacity. 'Mark?' she said, grabbing at his arm. 'Dominic, Mark's out there!'

He was watching her with a flat unwinking gaze. 'Yes, I know.'

Beneath her clutching hand his arm was smooth and solid, the muscles flexing slightly. Swallowing again to ease the harsh dryness in her throat, she strove for calm. 'How long before it hits?' she asked huskily.

His hand came to cover hers in a grip that held her trembling fingers still. 'First of all, it's not carved in stone that it's going to get here. If there's one thing that we do know about cyclones it's that they almost never do what they're supposed to. And secondly, Pihaia's been dealing with all the weather that Fala'isi can offer for over sixty years. He knows the signs of a cyclone, so he'll be hustling the boys back as fast as he can.'

She nodded, her eyes fixed imploringly on him. 'Yes, of course. But if it does come, and if he doesn't get them back—what then?'

Not a muscle moved in his face. He said calmly, 'Odds are they'll survive it. An atoll only a few feet above sea level may not seem very much shelter, but the Polynesians have had thousands of years learning how to cope with cyclones. If the worst comes to the worst he'll tie them to the trees above the reach of the waves. At the very least they'll have a better chance than anyone who's caught at sea.'

The colour drained from her face, leaving her sallow and drawn, desperately clinging to her self-control. 'And if they set out too late? If they're still on the sea when it hits?'

Dominic could have tried to fob her off with platitudes, lied to her, given her what she so desperately wanted to hear, but he didn't. That was not his way. 'If they're in the boat they'll have very little chance of surviving. But Pihaia will have taken that into consideration. You can safely leave their welfare to him. In the meantime,' he said, 'you can go and pack.'

'Pack?'

He nodded, his face carved from copper as he told her, 'I'm sending Grandfather back to Australia in the Learjet, and you're going with him.'

'Don't be a fool! I'm not going without Mark.'

In a voice that made the hair in the back of her neck lift he said evenly, 'You're going with Grandfather to Sydney.'

Fenella's fingers clenched on to his arm, digging painfully into the flexed muscles. 'No,' she whispered entreatingly. 'Please!'

He didn't move, and she knew that neither tears nor pleading would move him. She drew a deep breath, striving for courage. 'I'll do anything else you want me to, I promise, but I can't leave. Mark is my brother—I have the right to stay.'

'Have you ever been in a cyclone?' Dominic spoke curtly, not attempting to hide his irritation. At her quick headshake he said, 'I have. Please go with Grandfather, Fenella. I'm going to have enough to worry about without wondering what the hell's happening to you.'

'Are you staying?'

He looked at her without relenting. 'Yes. But you have no choice. You're going if I have to tie you up and put you on the bloody plane myself.'

'But Mark——'

'You can't do anything for him by staying here, and if the cyclone hits you're going to be nothing but a damned nuisance,' he told her brutally.

Fenella went white, her hand dropping to her side. Numbed, she realised that that was exactly how he saw her, how he had always seen her, a damned nuisance.

'Go and get your things ready,' he said curtly.

Fenella gave in because she could see that he was adamant. If necessary he would make good his threat. She even drove with James and a calmly competent Peter Brown to the airport in a taxi, answering James's grumbles with a set smile and enough wry teasing to make him smile. He was not in the least happy about being banished, but he accepted that Fala'isi with a cyclone on the way was no place for him.

Staring out of the window, Fenella wished she could accept Dominic's decision with such compliance. Her gaze brooded over the scurry of activity all the way to the airport. It was obvious that the news had been efficiently carried right around Fala'isi. The Islanders, smiles no longer in evidence, hurried about making ready for the onslaught. Anger, and a cold determination, stiffened Fenella's resolve. She was not going to be sent away as a refugee, not when Mark was in danger.

All right, so she couldn't do anything for him, as Dominic had so cruelly pointed out, but she could make sure she was not a nuisance, and to have to wait in Australia for news would kill her.

When she had seen James Maxwell on the small jet she walked back down on to the tarmac and said with a painful but determined smile to Peter Brown, 'I'm sorry, I can't leave without Mark. Tell Mr Maxwell I'll get a taxi back to the house, and that I'll be sensible.'

He tried to change her mind, but he was no Dominic, and when one of the men on the sleek little jet came to the top of the steps and called a warning to hurry up he gave up, warning her as he went back to this charge, 'Dominic's not going to be at all happy with this, miss.'

'I know. Never mind.'

She was just getting into a taxi when she saw the silver plane take off, flying with swift sureness south, away from the deadly stormclouds that were already massing behind the mountains in the north-east.

The trip back to the house was slow and difficult. The roads were crowded with people whose road sense seemed to have fled with the news of the oncoming cyclone. The young driver of the taxi at first regaled her with horrific tales of past storms and the damage they had done, but before long he lapsed into silence, clearly longing to get back to his village.

When at last they reached Maxwell's Reach Fenella paid him off and with head held high went into the house, to find Mari supervising the maids as they taped windows and moved furniture into the centre of the room. The rooms were bare and bleak; all the ornaments had been packed away in cupboards. Outside, a couple of youths were dragging the terrace furniture into a sturdy shed behind the garage.

'I thought you were going on the plane,' the house-keeper said blankly. 'Back to Australia.'

Fenella shook her head, her expression set in stubborn lines. 'No. Mark is here.'

Mari's aristocratic face tightened. 'Mr Dom's gone for them in the cruiser,' she said. She glanced out of the window, rubbing away a strand of hair that had stuck to her temple. 'With three of the fathers. If that stupid cyclone holds off for a little bit longer they should be back soon.'

'Why didn't he take the helicopter?' But even as she asked she knew why.

'Not enough room,' Mari said succinctly, casting an uneasy glance through the windows that overlooked the lagoon.

It didn't look as though Peta was going to hold off. At that moment the hazy sun disappeared behind the roiling clouds that had been creeping up from the horizon, and the sticky wind moaned around the eaves. The heat was intolerable, a pall of suffocating humidity.

'Well, you might as well make yourself busy while you wait. Can you check to make sure all the shutters are closed?' Mari said briskly. She hesitated. 'I'm going back to my family in Avanui, and the girls are coming with me. You better come too, we've got our new hall that's built of concrete, Dom says it will keep us all safe.'

Fenella shook her head. That would be just as bad as waiting for news in Australia. Besides, she didn't want Mari burdened with the responsibility of her safety. 'No, I'll wait for them here.' At the housekeeper's doubtful glance she insisted, 'I'll be perfectly all right. I won't do anything stupid.'

'They might not get here,' Mari said bluntly.

Fenella went white but spoke without a tremor in her voice. 'I'll be perfectly all right, this place is solid enough to withstand any number of cyclones—Dominic said so.'

Mari directed another haunted look outside, obviously eager to get back to her family in Avanui.

'You'd better go,' said Fenella.

Mari nodded. 'All right, though I don't know what Dominic will say about it. Whatever happens, stay inside. There's food in the esky——'

Fenella looked her astonishment and the housekeeper permitted herself a sardonic smile. 'You New Zealanders call them chillybins. I've filled them with enough food for three or four days. There's coffee and cold drinks in the thermos.'

'Thank you.' Fenella scarcely knew what she was saying.

Mari paused again. 'No, you better come with us. What if they don't get back? You don't know——'

'I'll stay here just the same.' She warded off the prospect of Mark and Dominic not coming back with a curious little movement of her hands. 'I won't go outside until the cyclone has gone, I promise.'

Mari gave her a hard look, her mouth compressed. 'Don't go near any of the windows in case they blow in, and don't go outside until someone comes for you. All right?'

'Yes. Thank you.'

One of the maids popped her head around the corner, eyes widening visibly when she saw Fenella. She said something in Maori to Mari, who looked uneasily from one to the other. With a sinking heart Fenella realised that Dominic had been right, she was nothing but a nuisance.

'You'd better go,' she told her again.

Mari hovered. 'Lock the door behind me, and don't use the electricity, and don't go near the windows. And *stay inside*. If they don't come back, stay inside until the radio tells you it's OK to go outside. If the roof starts to come off open the windows on the side away from the wind,' she ordered with a brisk practicality that chilled Fenella's blood. 'Don't have a bath or a shower. And don't eat too much—you don't know how long it's going to be before we can get fresh food. But make sure you stay inside.'

The sick fear in Fenella's stomach was like cramp, a physical nausea. She nodded. 'I'll be sensible.'

'You better be,' Mari said darkly. 'I don't know what Dominic's going to do to me for leaving you here, but I know he'll skin you alive when he gets back. He doesn't like people who don't do what they're told!'

On which dire threat she left, hurrying off through the rising wind that moulded her graceful cotton *muumuu* against her ample form.

Fenella waited until she was out of sight before setting off to check the shutters. A quick survey of the house revealed that the place was barricaded as tightly as a castle ready to repel a siege. In spite of the security of the new hall at Avanui, Fenella decided she would back

Maxwell's Reach to last through the worst the Pacific could offer.

Seizing the pair of high-powered binoculars that normally stood on the seaward terrace, she ignored Mari's injunctions to stay inside and made her way there. The storm was approaching fast. The wind had begun to whip the fronds of the coconut palms about, tossing them high into the air, picking up bits of dead leaves and debris and whirling them away. The waves on the reef roared thunderously in her ears, a harsh din that echoed in her heart. Even as she watched she realised that the breakers were coming faster and faster, their shattering demise pluming spray high into the wild air.

Staring out across the turbulent water, she willed the Maxwells' big cruiser to appear, her heart a cold lump in her breast as she realised that the sea, so merciless, so implacable, held in its clutches all that was dear to her.

Already the ocean was a mass of foaming waves, white and churning. Peta was preparing his attack on the island. The wind snatched greedily at her hair, flattened her clothes against her body. Almost gasping with the force of it, Fenella stood with her eyes closed, praying.

It seemed like a miracle when she opened them and there, making for the dangerous gap opposite Avanui, was the cruiser cutting through the cruel sea. The wind tore her yell of triumph away, and instantly she fell silent again, watching with strained eyes and ice in her veins as the big vessel powered down on to the passage, ignoring the huge waves that were beginning to break against the reef.

'I can't bear to watch,' she muttered, but she did. 'Please, let him have found the boys,' she begged beneath her breath. 'Please!'

Whoever was at the helm was a superb sailor. For a second the big boat hung back, seemingly losing way, until it caught a huge wave and surfed in through the narrow passage. Fenella moaned, but the cruiser surged

up through the welter of foam and with a quick turn
headed across the angry water towards Avanui.

The wind was beginning to scream in the palms, but
Fenella stayed watching until the cruiser disappeared
from sight behind the headland.

Then she lowered the binoculars, but although she
knew she should go inside she couldn't move. Not until
she knew whether Mark was on the cruiser, or whether
he and the other boys she had seen leave with such high
spirits a few days ago were still out there in that maelstrom of storm and fury, fighting for their lives.

Surely the boys were on it—otherwise, why go first to
Avanui? But no, Mari had said that Dominic had some
of the fathers with him.

Cramps knotted her stomach, fear like a deadly weight
took up residence there. If it was humanly possible
Dominic would have found them, she told herself
sturdily.

Would they stay at the village, or would they return
to Maxwell's Reach? And if they did, would they come
overland, surely by far the safer way? Knuckles clenching
whitely at her sides, she kept vigil for ten minutes or so
until to her incredulous joy the cruiser reappeared,
charging across the savage waters of the lagoon with what
seemed to be a reckless disregard for coral heads. But
of course Dominic knew the lagoon like the back of his
hand.

The wind stung her skin and forced her eyes into slits,
rising to a crescendo that seemed like the wail of a
thousand animals, and then rising yet again in an eerie,
devilish scream. Terrified, yet awed by the ferocious
majesty of nature at its most untamed, she watched un-
believingly as waves began to force their way over the
reef. As yet they died to nothing in the vast expanse of
the lagoon, but soon they would come right up to the
beach, barely tamed by the reef.

Clinging to the support of the terrace, Fenella realised
that she would have to go inside. The solid limestone
blocks of the house stood foursquare to the battering

force of the wind, but coconuts by the score crashed to the ground in a deadly hail, and another fear caught at her heart. How were Mark and Dominic going to run that gauntlet without being bombed by the lethal nuts?

Always supposing Mark—— A low cry of relief, of unutterable joy broke from her lips as she saw the two figures on the cruiser.

Hot tears scorched down her cheeks. Sniffing, she scrubbed them away, but it was some minutes later before she could clearly see the two men were running through the palms as fast as they could, Mark's slender figure sheltered from the worst of the wind—and from the deadly rain of coconuts—by Dominic's lithe strong form. An arm protected each beloved head, and, she realised with a sudden spurt of fury, each face was creased in an identical grin of pure, masculine recklessness.

A grin that was wiped from both faces when they saw her clinging to the terrace supports.

'Get inside, you stupid little bitch!' Roughly Dominic dragged her from her station, hauling her along the terrace and into the protection of the garage. 'Come on, before things get really rough.'

Once inside he stared down at her with fury flaming deep in the pale eyes. 'I couldn't believe it when Mari came tearing down to tell me you were still here. I thought I told you to go,' he said through his teeth.

Fenella's eyes devoured Mark's wet, excited face. 'I had to stay.'

Dominic's hands clenched. He looked down at them as though they belonged to someone else, paused, then turned away. 'See that Mark gets into dry clothes,' he ordered brusquely. 'Is everything else done? Water in the baths, food prepared?'

'Yes. Mari did all that before she left.' But she couldn't leave it at that. She went on swiftly, 'Dominic, they will be safe in Avanui, won't they?'

His smile was a narrow white line, savage, underlining the fact that he hated the sensation of helplessness. 'They'll be as safe as we are,' he said abruptly. 'I suggested they come here, but they built the hall for just such an emergency, and I had an engineer check out the plans. The place should stand through Armageddon! It will last, unless we get something we've never experienced before. Mark, get those damned clothes off!'

Grinning, Mark kissed Fenella with damp affection before disappearing.

Dominic stared a moment longer at her, the lines and planes of his face tightened in brutal anger. Then he too left, striding arrogantly out of the room.

Lacing her shaking fingers together, Fenella sank into a chair, waiting for them to come back.

They joined her in the weird twilight of the shuttered sitting-room, Dominic dry now in dark blue trousers and a pale beige shirt with sleeves rolled up to reveal the swarthy skin of his arms, Mark in jeans and a T-shirt. It was still stuffy and hot inside, although outside the wind howled mercilessly.

Dominic said evenly, 'The water in the baths is not to wash in, it's to drink. We may well have no clean water for days except that, so use it frugally.'

Fenella couldn't prevent herself from stiffening defensively as he came across the room with that silent predator's gait, smooth and infinitely dangerous.

'Yes, you should look wary,' he said as he sat down beside her, 'but you can save it for a while. We'll discuss your direct disobedience when the cyclone is over.'

A particularly vicious blast of wind tore at the fabric of the house, sending more coconuts crashing on to the ground.

'I don't owe you obedience,' she parried, watching as he leaned his head back on the sofa, the blunt angles and straight lines of his face accentuated by tiredness.

His mirthless smile frightened her. 'Don't you believe it, lady,' he said. 'Did Grandfather get off safely?'

'Yes, I saw the Learjet take off in plenty of time.'

'Good.' His lashes closed, making shadows on the bronze skin of his cheeks.

Fenella's heart gave an odd thump. Out on the terrace, waiting for her first sight of the cruiser, she had realised that she loved this complex, difficult man, loved him quite desperately, had loved him perhaps since she was sixteen. He had risked his life to go out and bring back Mark and the others, and he had done it without thought of reward. But that was not why she loved him. It was something quite different, a kind of elemental recognition, as though she had been doomed to love him since birth.

Her mouth curved in a faint, bitter smile. Because of course he didn't love her. Oh, he wanted her, but the tenderness and affection, the quiet sweetness of love, that was not there. And without that the feral fire, the elemental untamed passion, was not worth very much even though it promised raptures unbearable.

Mark came over to sit beside her, squashing her against Dominic's hard thigh.

'What about the helicopter?' he asked. 'Will it be all right?'

Dominic's wide shoulders lifted. 'It's well lashed down in its hangar. It'll have to take its chances like the cruiser.'

'I don't see how it can get much worse,' Mark commented after a particularly violent gust screamed around the buildings.

'It will.' Dominic's lashes stayed obdurately down.

Mark's eyes rounded. 'Gosh,' he said inadequately. 'What's it going to be like when we're in the middle of it?'

'Unpleasant. It gets worse and worse and worse, until you think there's no way it can possibly get worse. But it does. And then things start to go downhill.' Dominic turned his head so that he could see both of them through his narrowed eyes. 'And then it gets worse again. The house has withstood several other cyclones, but this one might be the biggest we've had since we built the place. If I tell you to do something,' his eyes rested deliberately on Fenella's pale face, 'you do it, all right? Stupidity on your part could well endanger other lives.'

She nodded, her skin pinkening suddenly.

'Cross my heart,' she said, trying to lighten the clammy tension with the childish phrase.

'Yes, of course,' said Mark when his half-brother's intimidating gaze moved to him.

Dominic's teeth gleamed for a second in the dusky room, but it was no smile. 'Not that anything should happen,' he said calmly. 'We're well above sea level, and the winds will be coming for the most part from the other direction so the storm surge shouldn't reach us, but if it does we're going to have to get out of here.'

'You mean we're actually sheltered from the worst of it?' Fenella's voice was level, but she had to work to make it that way. It seemed impossible that the cacophony outside could get any worse.

'Yes, it's coming in from the east, and theoretically we should be a lot safer than the few settlements on that side of the island. But mountains can play tricks with a cyclone. Sometimes the contours of the hills and the speed and direction of the winds combine to lower the air pressure in the lee of the mountains, causing furious gusts of wind to hurtle down the valleys, gusts that can rip the roof off. If that happens we'll have to open the windows on the leeward side to ease the air pressure.'

He paused, and both Mark and Fenella nodded, their faces solemn.

He resumed, 'In the middle of the cyclone quite possibly there'll be a period of calm, even blue skies.'

'The eye.' Mark's knowledgeable tone made Fenella hide a wry little smile.

'Yes, the eye. More people have been killed by going out into the eye of a hurricane than at any other time. So stay inside.'

Fenella and Mark both nodded.

Dominic held her eyes for a second longer, then relaxed. 'Just so you know,' he said, and leaned back into the seat. He had to be exhausted, making that mad dash across a wild sea to save Mark.

Fenella eyed the thermos flask of coffee, but on second thoughts decided it might be better to save it for later.

'Tell me what happened to you,' she said, turning to Mark.

'Well, when we woke up this morning Pihaia told us to get ready to come back because he knew the cyclone had turned our way.'

'How?'

Mark said earnestly, 'It's really incredible, you know. He could tell from the way the waves hit on the reef, and the sky, and the fact that it was so hot. But he'd listened to the radio he had tucked away somewhere, and Radio Fala'isi confirmed his suspicions. Believe me, we got ready in a hurry, and by the time the sun came up we were on the water. The sunrise was absolutely beautiful, with a scarlet sky—apparently that's another sign. We made for home as fast as we could, paddling like Olympic eights champions, with Pihaia and Turoa listening over the bow, reading the sea. I don't know how they do it, but it certainly made them worried! They said the cyclone was on its way and moving fast.'

'It's believed the Polynesians originally came from Asia.' Dominic's voice was deep and even, apparently unaffected by strain or tiredness. 'If they hadn't been able to read the sea and the skies they'd never have got as far as this. The Pacific is huge and dangerous, yet they managed to settle almost every small scrap of land between Fiji and and South America, as far south as New Zealand and north to Hawaii. Thousands must have been lost over the centuries, perhaps hundreds of thousands, but they're still here, still flourishing, still probably the best sailors the world has ever known. It took the coming of the Europeans two hundred years ago to give them their greatest setback.'

Fenella nodded. The history of European exploration in the South Seas was a mixture of incredible courage and great cruelty, but the most dangerous peril to the Polynesians had been the childhood diseases Europeans were almost immune to. Hundreds of thousands had died of measles and chickenpox, influenza and mumps, an appalling tragedy that wasn't yet over. Even in New Zealand with its excellent public health system, Maori children died of diseases that their *pakeha* counterparts survived with ease.

'Where did you meet the cruiser?' she asked her brother.

Mark grinned. 'About an hour off the island. Talk about the cavalry! I think Pihaia had decided it was quite possible we weren't going to be able to get to Fala'isi before the cyclone struck, because we were heading for another little *motu* on the horizon. I suppose he hoped we'd ride it out there. Then Dom came over the horizon like the marines, the cruiser stretched full out, flying along with a bone in her teeth.'

He aired his newfound nautical terminology with a pride that made Fenella hide another smile. 'What does that mean?'

'A curling wave at the bow. It looks like a bone from the front. I can tell you, I was pleased to see him. The sea was awfully lumpy and I was feeling a bit green, as well as being distinctly nervous about our chances. Anyway, Dom came to a screeching halt beside us, ordered us in, and then we just let Pihaia's boat go.'

'Oh, the poor man!'

'He didn't say no, although he looked a bit sick. But boy, what a trip back!' Mark grinned past her, hero-worship shining in his countenance. 'Dom must believe the cruiser's a plane, he had her nearly flying most of the way. We came in through the gap in the reef like a surfboard.'

'I know.' Fenella repressed a shudder. 'I saw you.'

'It was great,' Mark boasted.

Another blast of wind harried the house. From outside there was a sudden horrendous crash, followed by another.

'A tree coming down,' said Dominic. 'On to the generator house, by its direction.'

'The power's turned off,' Fenella told him. 'Mari did that before she left.'

He nodded, then began to tell them about the first white settler who had arrived on Fala'isi, the great-great-grandfather of the man who was still the paramount chief.

'His name was Grant Chapman,' he said.

Fenella made a little sound and he grinned. 'Yes— Grant is a direct descendant. His ancestor arrived on a trading vessel when nearly everyone on the island had been killed by disease or the sandalwood traders, or the trepang fishers. Only one chief was left, and he was dying of the measles. But he had a beautiful daughter, a sacred virgin . . .'

He was a brilliant storyteller, his deep, beautiful voice superbly equipped to tell such a tale. As the cyclone brought its impossible force to bear on the island they sat in the dark humid room and strained to hear while he told them of a hero, a strong, ruthless, not too scrupulous Englishman, and an arrogant, wilful, incredibly beautiful Polynesian princess who was the heroine, of villains in assorted sizes and cunning, tempests, earthquakes, tidal waves, warfare and treachery, a forced marriage and the slow, reluctant awakening of love.

It was the kind of tale that had kept mankind's ancestors fascinated for years around a cave fire, that still sold millions in brightly covered novels. The kind of tale almost guaranteed to keep terrified people's minds off what was happening beyond the cave entrance, through the beleaguered city walls, outside in the hurricane.

'Oh, man, what a story!' Mark had to wait until a particularly vicious blast of wind eased a little before he could make himself heard. 'And their descendants still live here?'

'Not very far away.' Dominic grinned reminiscently. 'The genes are still strong. Grant Chapman probably wouldn't thank you for saying it, but he'd agree that the first Chapman wasn't much more than a pirate, although one with a few more morals than most. Grant's got a touch of the buccaneer in him still, for all that he looks like a French aristocrat and talks like an Englishman.'

And you, Fenella thought, are another such one. Some note in his voice, some hint of fellow-feeling, revealed that Dominic would have liked to sail the unknown Pacific over a hundred years ago with nothing but his wits and his strong right arm to rely on.

She could imagine him doing it too; he had the authority and the daring to settle on an island and make it his.

But that sort of derring-do was denied men now; they had to find other ways of satisfying their urge to explore, to carve out a dominion of their own. Perhaps that was why the world of business had become a substitute battle field, somewhere they could sublimate the warlike instincts bred in them over the generations of bloody heritage.

Her eyes lingered on Dominic's blunt, autocratic profile, following the stubborn, angular chin, the high forehead and the curved, sensuous line of his mouth, sculpted cleanly against the copper skin. He was alarmingly good-looking, yet oddly enough it was not his looks that made him impressive. Quite simply he had presence, this man she loved. Presence and authority, and a kind of basic, rock-hard integrity.

He said quietly, 'Let's go and see what's happening.'

The three of them—for Mark got eagerly to his feet—went through the house. When they reached a window overlooking the sea and peered through the shutters, a scene of such desolation met their eyes that Fenella gave a soft little moan of anguish.

Waves were boiling over the reef and surging right up to the beach, smashing down with all the force of surf on a weather shore, their monstrous forms grey with debris and sand. The lagoon was a battlefield where huge combers roaring through the passage met the storm waves in the lagoon to explode in a fury of foam.

Between the house and the beach coconut palms lay in heaps, tangled and broken, torn out by the roots. Great branches had been hurled across the lawn and the gardens, and the whole area was littered with huge drifts of leaves, driving steadily before the shrieking wind. Even as they watched, another coconut palm succumbed to the power of the wind; Fenella's eyes were darkened by tears as she watched the tortured palm lurch to the ground. And the truly terrifying thing about it was that although she felt it with every fibre of her being she couldn't hear its death throes through the scream of the wind.

Surely nothing could be worse than this, yet she was surprised to hear Dominic say, 'Not too bad. Let's have a look at the other side.'

Not a word escaped from any of them at the sight of the carnage on the other side. The mountains were hidden by the driving rain and the seething mass of clouds, but although Maxwell's Reach was protected from the full force of the wind the destruction was incredible, trees and plants in a wild tangle across what had yesterday been gardens, the pool full of debris, screens flattened, and that tidal wave of leaves and debris choking up the garden beds and the lawns.

Fenella bit her lip. 'What's happening in Fala'isi?' she asked. 'The town, I mean. It must be almost directly in the path of the wind.'

Dominic slanted a thoughtful look in her direction, then took her hand, his own reassuringly big and warm around her cold fingers. 'It will be getting a pasting,' he said, not sparing her, 'but it will survive. They build for these cyclones here, and the people know what to do about them. What worries me is the river there. If it rises too high they may have trouble.'

The long day stretched on with the violent uproar continual around them. During one particularly savage onslaught the roof creaked and they froze, but it held. They drank coffee and ate the cold lunch that Mari had left, and some time after their sketchy dinner Fenella even slept a little. But she woke a little later, her every nerve jumping, her heart thudding with a fear she couldn't recognise.

'What——'

'Shh!' Dominic's voice was soft in her ear.

And she realised that she could hear him, that there was silence outside except for the roar of the sea. With eyes attuned to the darkness she stared around the elegant room. Mark had chosen to stretch out on the other sofa; she could see his dark head against the pale fabric.

And she was curled up in Dominic's arms, her head resting trustfully against his chest, her legs inside his, in a position of complete trust.

'Is it over?' she whispered joyously.

'No. It's the eye.'

The stillness was uncanny.

'Come and have a look,' said Dominic, easing her off the sofa so that he could swing his long legs down.

Fenella should have been embarrassed by finding herself in such a position, but it seemed right, somehow, just as it seemed right that she should let her hand lie in his as they made their way across to the window.

Outside the dark day had long gone, swallowed up by an even darker night.

'There are stars,' she whispered. 'Look, Dominic.'

'If it was daytime we'd be seeing the sun.'

She shuddered. Of all the uncanny things that had happened that long day this seemed to be the strangest. To look out and see stars, and know that the island was surrounded by belts of cyclonic winds shutting it off from the rest of the world.

And then she heard the wind coming across the wild sea, screaming with the fury of death, shrieking over the lagoon and on to them, its arrival like a punch in the stomach. The stars vanished. It seemed that the whole house shuddered, and Fenella stiffened, waiting for the crack of tiles lifting, the sound of the roof tearing free to leave them exposed to the full savagery of the cyclone.

'It's all right.' Dominic's voice was astonishingly matter-of-fact. 'This house was built for anything the wind can throw at it.'

Sighing, Fenella relaxed against him, all fear fled, aware that deep in some purely instinctive part of her she trusted this man as she had trusted no other. He might be hard and dominating, too arbitrary for a modern woman, but when he said that things were all right, she believed him.

'Come on,' he said above the banshee howl of the wind. 'See if you can sleep some more.'

Meekly she went back into the dark room and sank with him on to the sofa, holding him as he was holding her, two humans who had had it forcibly brought home to them just how puny they were in Nature's eyes.

She didn't sleep much during the rest of the night, and towards dawn she realised with incredulous joy that the wind was easing, the violent gusts coming further and further apart, the force slowly fading.

By dawn she was certain of it. Unable to guess whether Dominic was awake or not, she moved gingerly, but he said, 'Lie still.'

'Have you slept at all?'

'In snatches.'

She looked up into his beloved face, seeing no weariness in the strong lines. 'Is this the end, or just another calm?'

'The end.' His mouth twisted. 'Unless the bloody thing turns around and backtracks, of course.'

'Pessimist!'

'Realist,' he corrected, smiling grimly. 'It's highly unlikely, although it has happened.'

Fenella looked across to where Mark lay curled up, still sleeping peacefully. 'I didn't thank you for going out to get them yesterday,' she began, her voice wobbling as she thought of the group of boys and one old man forced to see out that maelstrom of nature on a small atoll only a few feet above the sea.

'You don't have to.'

Pulling herself free, she knelt on the sofa, looking at him. 'Yes, I do. I didn't expect you to——'

'I chose to go,' he said, cutting her short with an impatient gesture. 'I would have gone even if Mark hadn't been in the group.'

'Yes, I know,' she said softly, her eyes filling with tears. 'It was crazy—but magnificent.'

He lifted his brows, mocking her choice of words. 'Whereas you, Fenella, are still in deep trouble for disobeying me.'

She grinned. 'So punish me.'

'I'm thinking of a suitable one, believe me.' The words were a soft threat, the smile that touched his hard mouth promised painful retribution. 'But in the meantime, do you think you can produce some sort of breakfast while I check around the house? Make it a good sustaining one, because it's going to be a hell of a day.'

It was. After breakfast the wind had died away enough for him to make his way over to Avanui. He met her offer to accompany him with a brusque refusal that stung even after she realised that he had no idea what the hazards of the path were likely to be.

He arrived back an hour later as she and Mark were busy pushing the furniture back into place and returning the lamps and pictures, the ornaments and decorations.

'Everyone's OK there. The hall held, although they had one or two bad moments with the roof,' he said shortly, 'but I've checked on the radio and they need the helicopter. Things don't sound too good in the town and the outer islands.'

'I'll come too,' said Mark, eagerness lighting up his face. 'I can help you navigate. Is the helicopter OK?'

'Yes, but you're not coming.' Dominic stopped his protests with devastating curtness. 'I'll be taking a doctor and any extra space will be filled with medical supplies.'

Mark was crestfallen, but he nodded. 'Oh, of course— I didn't think.'

'See what you can do here, then go on over to Avanui and help them tidy up,' he commanded as he strode out of the door. 'Be careful going through the trees—I've cut a path through, but some of it may be treacherous.'

Fenella bit her lip. He had not even looked at her as he left, as though those hours spent in his arms had meant nothing.

Of course, nothing was exactly what they had meant, she thought, turning to see what else she could do. Merely the elemental comfort derived from the closeness of another human being. And she had better not forget it.

Like Mark, she wanted to be able to help, to do something, but when she made her way through the tangle of uprooted and smashed jungle to Avanui and asked Mari what she could do, she was told that everything was under control. As indeed it appeared to be. The villagers were putting their wrecked buildings back together again, singing as they worked, their lovely mellow voices blending in perfect harmonies. Fenella went to the chief and offered her help, but he refused it, telling her with a broad grin that she should go home and wait for her man, because he would be needing her.

She should have been furious. Every feminist instinct should have bristled at the thought of being anyone's woman. But she had liked the sound of it. Oh, you fool, she thought, listening to Mari's instructions on what she and Mark could do at Maxwell's Reach.

Together they began to clear away the debris, working from the house out, plugging away steadily in spite of the appalling heat and humidity.

Mark emerged from the generator house flushed with triumph at his success in getting it to go, so they had electricity, which relieved Fenella's mind of worry about the contents of the deep-freeze; this should have provided them with water too, from the two huge concrete tanks behind the house. Indeed, water did flow from the kitchen tap, but it was muddy, so she decided to continue using the water in the baths in case the supply had been contaminated.

By the time the abrupt dusk had fallen again the terrace was cleared of its pall of leaves and sticks and twigs.

She had washed the mud from the tiles with a bucket and broom, and she and Mark had cleaned the windows of their thick layer of salt.

The intermittent rain that had followed the cyclone had gone, and the sky was clear and calm as the sun went down, the air soft and moist and refreshing.

'Well, this is more like it,' Fenella remarked as they drank tea after a substantial dinner. 'We'll feel more like working when we've had a decent night's sleep.'

'I wonder where Dominic is.'

She had been wondering that too, but she said briskly, 'I dare say he'll be back when they have no further reason to use the helicopter. You'd better go to bed, love; that yawn nearly broke your face in two, and we'll have another busy day tomorrow.'

He was exhausted, but he wanted to wait up with her for Dominic; it wasn't until she pulled rank that he finally gave in and took himself grumbling off to his room.

CHAPTER EIGHT

OUT on the terrace Fenella waited in the darkness for the sound of the helicopter to override the now much quieter note of the waves as they crashed on to the reef. It seemed impossible that only a few hours earlier those waves had been thundering on to their beach, and even more astonishing that so little damage had been done to it. Apart from seaweed and shards of coral, the sand was as smooth as it had ever been.

It was a different story on land. Trees and palms lay heaped up in wild tangles, their roots held pleadingly to a pitiless sky.

Fenella sighed, her eyes scanning the sky, serene now that the last of the wind had died away. Another hazy night; the stars glimmered with haloes through a thin veil of cloud. About as different as it could be from the chaos of the preceding one.

From the radio she had learned so far that the death toll had been light on Fala'isi, but on the atolls to the north and the low islands to the west there had been much more destruction, more deaths. Food and medical supplies were being ferried out to them, seriously injured people were being brought to the mainland. An Air Force Hercules from New Zealand and another from Australia were on their way with much-needed supplies.

She had almost decided to go to bed when she heard the throb-throb-throb of the helicopter coming in fast and low across the discoloured waters of the lagoon. It landed, and still she waited for Dominic to arrive.

At last, made uneasy by the fact that he hadn't arrived, she set off towards the helipad, picking her way along the track with the aid of one of the torches, black brows drawn together. She was almost up to the helicopter before she saw him, still in the chopper, speaking into the radio.

' . . . be coming on the Learjet here tomorrow,' he said in a infinitely weary voice, then was silent.

Fenella stepped back, closing her ears. He said a few more words and that was the end of the conversation. But he didn't get out of the cockpit. When she looked up he was still in the pilot's seat, his big body sprawled back, a hand massaging a stiff neck.

'Dominic,' she said.

'Turn that torch off!' he snarled.

Hastily she redirected the beam on to the ground, but not before she had seen his face—filthy, with a thin bloody stripe down one cheek, his eyes bloodshot, it had revealed exactly what sort of day he had experienced.

Quietly she asked, 'Do you need a hand down?'

He stifled something that was probably an oath and said, 'Yes, I think I do.'

But as she moved towards the chopper door he decided to do without what poor help she could give him and half climbed, half fell from the door, his stagger as he reached the ground revealing more than anything else could have how exhausted he was.

'Come on,' she said quietly. 'I've got warmish water for a bath and some food waiting.'

He insisted she take the torch until she told him that it was well known that women saw better in the dark. Then he went in front of her, the wavering light of the beam revealing the fatigue that gripped him. Fenella's heart ached but, unsure of his reaction, she didn't offer sympathy.

Once in the house she couldn't prevent the small sound of horror she made when she scanned his face. Her shocked eyes took in the bruise darkening his cheekbone and the long abraded scratch down the left side of his face. But she noticed most of all the weariness that dulled the jade eyes to flat opacity, the dimming of the virile masculine vitality, that animal vigour that was so much a part of him.

Whatever he had been doing that long day he had pushed himself hard physically. He was swaying on his feet.

'They shouldn't have let you go on until you were exhausted,' she said harshly. Her hand went out. For a trembling second she touched the contusion, the line of dried blood on his cheek. He let her, watching her with empty eyes.

'Come on,' she commanded. 'Do you want to shower or bath?'

Dominic gave a ghost of a laugh. 'I'd like nothing better than to lie in a bath for twenty-four hours, but I doubt whether I'd ever be able to get out of it. I'd better have a shower.'

'OK. I'll heat some food for you and bring it to your room in twenty minutes.'

Something light and easily digested, yet nourishing. When in doubt, Fenella thought, trying to summon some humour, fall back on an omelette. After assembling the eggs she used the best bits of a lettuce she had found in the refrigerator to make a salad with avocado and the last good tomato. For a fruit salad she diced paw-paws and mangoes and bananas she had gathered more or less intact from the ruins of the garden.

All ingredients ready, she stood irresolute in the middle of the huge kitchen. She had heard nothing, but by then he should have had his shower and be ready for something to eat.

Before she could talk herself out of it she went along to his room and tapped on the door; at his muffled answer she opened it, to stop suddenly at the sight of him flat on his stomach across the huge bed, naked except for a towel draped casually across his buttocks.

'Are you all right?' she demanded, hurrying across the room.

Dominic turned his head towards her, but his eyes remained closed. 'I don't think I want anything to eat, there's a good girl,' he said offensively.

'Tough. I'm cooking an omelette.'

Opening his eyes, he surveyed her determined face, his smile a snarl. 'Feeling like Florence Nightingale? I don't need to be mothered.'

Fenella snapped, 'Believe me, if I'd been your mother you'd have a few more manners! I've assembled everything for the omelette, it won't take me a minute to make it, and you'll feel much better tomorrow morning if you eat something now.'

Seething, she hurtled out of the room and swished down the hall, all sympathy gone as she recapitulated the many reasons she had to dislike him.

The omelette turned out perfectly. Slapping it on to a plate and that on to a tray, she added the bowl of fruit salad and marched militantly back to his room, ready to make her feelings more than plain if he happened to make just one snide remark.

He still lay on the bed; as far as she could tell he hadn't moved. She put the tray down on the bedside table, said woodenly, 'I'll see you in the morning,' and left, her mouth dry at the sight of him sprawled as carelessly as a sunwarmed lion across the bed.

All the long, hot, exhausting day she had yearned for the moment when at last she could climb into bed. Now she was finally there her muscles relaxed, easing her into the coolness and freedom of the sheets. She stretched sinuously, but in spite of the hard day's work she had put in she didn't drop straight off. Instead she lay for a long time wondering what Dominic had been doing to make him so exhausted, so bone-weary, marked and cut by his labours.

Eventually, of course, she slept, but it could only have been a few hours before she was jerked awake by some sound. Her first thought was that the cyclone had doubled back on its tracks, but as she lay listening to the soft melodious call of the tree-frogs—how on earth had so many of them survived?—she realised that apart from the distant roar of the waves on the reef it was silent. No cyclone.

And no other sound either. Fenella was almost asleep again when she heard it once more, a choked contraction of noise, barely audible. She was out of her bed in an instant, dragging on the soft white satin robe, racing down the hall towards Mark's room.

But it wasn't Mark. The anguished, impeded sound came from Dominic's bedroom. For a moment she dithered, until she recalled the cut slashed down the side of his face and the bruise on his cheekbone.

Gingerly she tapped on the door, calling his name softly. No answer. Emotions riding high, she stole into the shadowed room, looking across to the bed. As she held her breath just inside the door he moved, a quick painful twist of the big sleek body, and a gasping plea, 'Oh, God, no!' was torn from his throat.

Fenella padded quietly across the room, stooping to touch his shoulder. She said his name and added soothingly, 'You're dreaming, Dominic. Wake up. It's just a dream.'

She knew the minute he woke up. It was like the dropping of a camera shutter; instantaneous. His hand flew out and caught her wrist, imprisoning her with a painful grip. Starlight shimmered in his eyes, picked out the slashing contours of his face. 'What is it?' he asked, his voice hoarse with sleep 'Sarah?'

She felt an utter fool, devastated by the sudden fierce pang that tore through her. 'You—called out. I thought—that is, I wondered——'

'Oh, God, not Florence Nightingale!' His eyes were closed again.

He was, she realised suddenly, afraid of what she might read there.

Putting aside her humiliation and pain, and the jealousy that corroded her heart, Fenella sat down on the edge of the huge bed and asked simply, 'What did you do today, Dominic?'

'Bullseye.' The word drawled out through lips that were too severely controlled. 'I flew rescue, and I picked up bodies. From along the beaches, from out at sea, and once from under what was left of a truck that had been trying to ford a river when the flood came down. Have you ever seen thirty-seven bodies laid out neatly in rows, Fenella? So many men, so many women, so many children. Two toddlers. And three babies. At first they were laid out separately, but when the relatives came to identify them they put them in family groups, the babies and children in their mothers' arms.' His grip on her wrist tightened, but she made no sound of protest. 'So much death, Fenella. I've seen it before, but it never loses its power to shock. Such empty husks, snuffed by a careless finger. And you come in here looking like every man's fantasies of life, with nothing on beneath satin that makes your skin look like a golden pearl, smooth and warm and gleaming.'

A quick flick and she was sprawled on top of him, with just the material of her robe between her and the supple torso, the long, heavily muscled legs, and the heated proof of his virility burgeoning beneath her.

Fenella should have been terrified, but to her astonishment the only emotion she was capable of feeling was an exhilaration that surged through her, setting fire to her nerves like sparks in straw. His hands cupped her face, pulling her down.

'You're so warm,' the beautiful smoky voice murmured. 'So sleek and smooth and warm, when I've been walking hand in hand with cold death all day. Warm me, Fenella. Give me something that will send me out to more death tomorrow knowing that there's still life, still beauty in the world.'

Perhaps it was because she was on top of him, perhaps that she had been so swiftly jerked from sleep that her inhibitions had been left behind; perhaps it was because she loved him, but the hollow exhaustion in his words and the anguish clouding his eyes made her ache with the desire to give him what ease it was in her power to do.

Perhaps this had been inevitable since he had kissed her when she was sixteen.

Murmuring his name in a soft, shaken voice, she kissed his face, her mouth lingering over the bruise on his cheekbone, pressing small kisses down the thin slash to his jaw. She could feel the tension, the ferocious control he was exerting; it was too much, he needed some sort of release, or else her powerful, forceful Dominic would crack from the pain.

Although he lay perfectly still she felt already taut muscles tighten further, the small shifts and flexions beneath the skin, the quiet desperation in his breathing.

Her mouth was soft and giving, almost tentative as she moulded the contours of his. She caught his hastily expelled breath in her mouth; he tasted of male, musk-sweet, salty, a dark masculine flavour that sent arrows of sensation singing along her nerves.

The hands that held her wrists prisoner relaxed, smoothing down her arms, slowly caressing her through the satin of the robe, while his mouth remained her toy, her plaything, hers to do with as she wished.

Emboldened, she flicked her tongue along the severe, sensual line of his lips, and when he didn't respond she whispered, 'Open for me, Dominic.'

She had indulged in this kind of deep kissing before, but always it had been the man who initiated the contact, who had taken her mouth, leaving her feeling as though she had been subtly violated.

This time it was she who wanted, she who took, her tongue touching his, relishing the wildfire reaction he couldn't hide, the involuntary contraction of the big body beneath her, the fine mist of sweat over the sleek copper skin. An explorer's fascination made her bold; she kissed him again, her body pulsing with a new, peculiar delight, and when his hands reached her shoulders she shuddered at the fine tremble in them as they smoothed up her back.

The heat of his touch through the fine satin caressed her skin to an instant sensitivity. Heat fountained up through her body, touching every tissue, warming her to a languor that was at once drowsy and violently, vividly alert.

'Satin lady,' he whispered against her seeking mouth. 'All that's sweet and desirable, my sweet satin woman. How did you know I needed this? Make me forget, Fenella. Give me something to hold on to in the cold reaches of the night when death seems so close and life is just a bitter joke.'

The beautiful voice ached with more than carnal need, a hunger she could understand; it almost made up for the fact that he was using her as a crutch. If this was all that she could give him, then she would. She too knew of times when life was nothing more than a bad joke and all she had wanted was someone to hold her and keep the ugliness and the uselessness of it away with the warmth of his body and the power of his caresses. Dominic had done that for her, held her in the sexless comfort of his embrace until she had stopped weeping.

For years she had wanted this man, been imprinted by him when she was scarcely more than a child. Now the desire was deeper, more basic: simple love, the desire to heal him, to give all of herself because she loved him. Oh, she hoped that in time he would realise he wanted her for much more than the easy surcease of his night terrors, but for now her instinct was to give him what he needed so much.

His hands moved gently down her back, smoothing over the fabric, until they reached her hips. There they tightened, forcing her against the hard virility of his loins, telling her without words what he wanted of her, what he needed.

Answering his question as silently, as candidly, she bent her head and kissed the strong line of his jaw, the length of his throat. Deep inside her the warmth and the hunger had ignited into something she had never experienced before, a fountain of honeyed fire, a rushing wind of sensation more powerful by far than the cyclone, for the cyclone could only destroy, and this was a storm of life and renewal.

Slowly, as though subconsciously he understood that this was new to her, he slipped the robe from her shoulders, pushing it down until she was exposed to the glittering green fire of his gaze, so concentrated that she had the fanciful thought it must be marking her skin, searing the pattern of his survey across her shoulders and the high firm globes of her breasts.

'You're so beautiful,' he murmured deeply. 'Soft and glowing and sensuous, sending out a message that you're not for just anyone, that the only man who deserves you is one prepared to struggle and suffer to possess you.'

Heat and colour suffused her skin, and her nipples peaked, desire pulling them into tight little buds.

Dominic laughed softly in his throat, thwarting her instinctive move to hide by the simple expedient of holding her away from him, his large strong hands dark against the smooth golden olive of her shoulders.

Shock and a kind of violent elation stopped her breath in her chest. She looked down into the drawn, hard face of a lover, a man with only instinct now, a man who was determined to take what he wanted, and for a terrifying moment it was like watching a stranger, a pirate intent on looting and violation.

Fenella's muscles froze; she whispered something, and the illusions wavered, then faded. It was Dominic who looked up at her, Dominic who gazed at her with such stark demanding hunger, and she loved him, she wanted him as much as he wanted her.

His hands on her shoulders gentled; slowly he lowered her, pulling her slightly to one side. He touched her waiting breast, long fingers darkly outlined against the soft flesh, and Fenella shivered, lost in a sensuous haze, the active logic of her brain overwhelmed by a more primitive, more fundamental need.

Her mouth shaped his name; he raised himself on a strong shoulder and kissed her, regaining the initiative in one driving movement as he made himself master of the sweetness of her mouth, taking it in a ferocious mastery. His hand shaped her breast, the thumb flicking

with gentle ownership over the budding nipple, sheer
sorcery, a magician's touch promising far more than it
gave, sending slivers of sharp delight boring through her
body.

Her backbone arched. He laughed deep and soft in
his throat and accepted the supple, instinctive invitation, his mouth closing around the aching point of her
breast, reassuring her that her decision to wait for this
had been the correct one, that Dominic was the only
man who had the right to claim her with this sensual
authority.

He made love to her with passion barely controlled
by his immense will, a hunger he managed to hold in
check for long enough to woo her into readiness with
hands and voice and mouth, the potent spell of his
maleness summoning a primal response from her fe-
maleness. For although she was transported into a voluptuous paradise by his loving, she stoked the fires with
her open, shy appreciation, her wonder at the way her
soft tentative touches galvanised his big body.

It gave her a heady feeling of power to know that she
could make him groan with pleasure, shake beneath the
sly caress of her hands, the open-mouthed kisses she
pressed on his skin, the way she followed his guidance
and suckled softly on the small male nipples, stroking,
exploring.

Then, when she thought that if he didn't take her she
might go mad with hunger, he moved over her and with
a steady thrust joined them. It hurt a little, but she looked
up into his drawn face, her hands pulling against the
bunched bulges of his muscles, and saw the immense
control he was using, and she relaxed, welcoming him.
With a muffled sound he pressed home, and Fenella discovered the ecstasy of union, the unbridled pleasure that
coursed through every cell in her body.

But that was nothing to what followed. Tossed by sen-
sations, she could only cling to him and follow where
he led, her untutored body responding to the demands
of his, discovering that in her surrender there was an

exhilaration that climbed, higher and higher, tighter and tighter, tensing her body as she sought for the unknown fulfilment, the longed-for completion.

Sweat slicked their bodies, yet still they clung, still the deep thrusts sent her soaring, until finally something snapped inside her and she cried out brokenly as she spun into ecstasy, drenched with sensation, lost in a storm of cataclysmic proportions that racked her, sensation and emotions blended into rapture.

She felt his body clench, every muscle lock, his head thrown back, and then he shuddered, a cry roughening his voice, and collapsed. For a precious few seconds she held him to her breasts as her heartbeat slowed and the world tilted back on to its axis. Too soon, he moved a little, scooping her sideways so that she lay half across him, and within seconds they were both asleep, lulled by the thunder of his heart under hers as the thudding blended into the thunder of the waves on the reef.

Fenella woke alone, and to the knowledge that whatever had happened last night was not likely to make any difference to the way he thought of her.

But oh, she thought, smiling faintly as she stretched her aching body across the huge bed, whatever happened now, it had been worth it. If she never touched another man in her life she would have her memories of the night to keep her warm.

When she had showered and dressed she went to check the helipad. It was empty. He had left her without a word, not even with a scrawled note. It hurt, but she told herself sturdily not to be a fool. Dominic would not let his personal affairs interrupt what he conceived to be his duty to the people of this lovely island when they needed him.

Trying to talk herself out of the faint feeling of betrayal, she peeped in on Mark. He was still lost in the solid sleep of adolescence.

Forcing a steady smile, she set about bringing more order to the house. Dominic's room first, she decided, with an odd falling sensation in her stomach. He could come back that night every bit as exhausted as he'd been the day before. Memories intruded, and she had to blink back the tears, but she kept going. She was standing with the sheet in her hand, lost in a sensual dream, when a movement at the door made her look up.

A woman in a wheelchair sat watching her, her expression colder, more contemptuous than ever Dominic's had been. She did not need to announce who she was; Dominic might have inherited the Maxwell features, but his colouring he got from his mother. Her skin bore the pallor of a life spent indoors, but the coppery undertone was there, as were the pale green eyes and the startlingly black lashes and brows.

Louise Maxwell.

'If you think that sleeping with my son is going to get you anything but a broken heart, then you're as big a fool as your mother,' the intruder said harshly. 'He told me to send you on your way.'

Fenella's hand clenched on to the sheet. 'I don't believe you,' she said uncompromisingly.

Another legacy from his mother had been Dominic's small cold smile. 'Really? What's the matter with you Gardner women, that you think you can rely on Maxwell men?' Louise permitted herself a small contemptuous sneer. 'A pair of naïve sluts, if there are such things. But I hope you won't commit suicide like your stupid mother. So messy. And so—vulgar. Trying to make them sorry. Well, Simon wasn't sorry, and Dominic won't be either.'

Fenella's head was held so high her neck ached. Grittily she returned, 'You can say what you like about me, but you'll leave my mother alone! She's dead, beyond anything your wretched husband and you can do to her.'

'Get your things packed!' Louise Maxwell's voice cracked like a whip. 'You're not wanted here.'

'I'm not going.'

The woman in the wheelchair looked at her. 'Then you'll just have to face Dominic himself when he gets back and finds you here,' she said spitefully. 'I doubt whether you'll want to stay when he's finished with you. And he has finished with you. He's engaged to a very suitable girl. Sarah's here too, waiting for me in the sitting-room.'

Sarah. The name Dominic had called in his sleep last night. Sarah Springfellow.

All Fenella's defiance oozed away like frost in the sun. So it was her arrival that Dominic had been organising in the helicopter last night. Betrayal, cold as death, hard as the ice in his eyes, stabbed Fenella's heart.

But she still held her head high. 'Dominic can tell me to go,' she said impassively.

'You stupid little fool, can't you see that he doesn't want you here?'

Probably not, Fenella thought drearily. But he had sent for Sarah before they had spent the night so rapturously together. Surely it had meant something to him? 'That's too bad,' she managed. 'If he doesn't want me here he can have the decency to tell me so himself instead of sending messages through his mother.'

'Suit yourself,' said Mrs Maxwell, shrugging her thin shoulders. 'It should be amusing for us all to see you get your come-uppance. And don't think that the nights you've spent in his bed are going to make any difference—either to him, or to Sarah. Men often sleep with women they despise, and Sarah knows that Dominic is probably not going to be faithful to her. Only romantic featherheads consider men to be faithful creatures. Sarah knows what to expect. She'll make him a good wife, provide him with children and act as his hostess.' She gave Fenella a slow contemptuous survey. 'She knows how to behave. She has breeding.'

A noise at the doorway caught both women's attention. Malice sparked deep in the pale eyes as a rumpled, yawning Mark appeared in the doorway.

'So this is the Maxwell bastard,' Louise said cruelly. 'Just as well he looks like the old man, isn't it, otherwise you'd have whistled in the wind for an ounce of attention. Hoping to make a fortune hanging off the

Maxwell sleeve, are you, boy? Forget it—the Maxwells don't bleed easily. Your slut of a mother found that out——'

'That will do!' Fenella went across to the door and pushed her brother out into the passage. 'Go and pack your things,' she commanded, ignoring his clenched fists and truculent expression. 'Go on!'

He hesitated, then fought back the fury, wordlessly turning back to his room. Waiting until the door had closed behind him, Fenella turned her head to meet the triumphant blaze in the older woman's eyes. 'You win,' she said through her teeth. 'I'll go.'

She could fight for herself, but she could not expose Mark to the dripping poison that was this woman.

Somehow she managed to get them both out of the house without meeting either Sarah Springfellow or Dominic's mother again. They arrived back in Auckland a weary seven hours later, and went straight to Fenella's flat. She had explained a little of what had happened to Mark, although she hadn't told him that she had spent the night before in Dominic's arms.

'OK,' he said, after brooding on it for a while, 'So what Mum did was wrong, but she didn't know that my father was already married, did she?'

Fenella sighed. 'I don't know,' she said honestly. 'We weren't that close, she and I, certainly not close enough for her to confide in me. But the Maxwells are sure she knew.'

'But she loved him, didn't she?'

'Oh, yes, she loved him. In her own way.' Had she really? Or had it been, as Dominic so cruelly said, merely a weak woman's dependence on a man?

He looked out across the wing at the limitless blue Pacific stretching beneath them all the way home, all the way back to Fala'isi. 'But the Maxwells don't believe that.'

'No, I'm afraid they don't.'

He said sturdily, 'I think my father was a swine.'

Fenella's eyes darkened. 'We don't know what made him do the things he did,' she said slowly. 'A tribe of American Indians have a proverb: I won't judge a man until I've walked all day in his moccasins. It seems a good idea to me.'

'I suppose so,' he said, clearly not convinced. 'Oh, well, I liked Dom very much, and Grandfather could be interesting too, but if they come complete with that old witch, I'd just as soon not see them again. She gave me the horrors.'

'She didn't do a lot for me either,' Fenella murmured, repressing a shudder.

Exhaustion clawed at her with sharp nails. Sooner or later she would pay the penalty for her folly of the night before, and the even greater folly of falling in love with a man who had only wanted to use her, but at the moment it didn't seem to be very important. She wanted only to go back to her flat and sleep for several days and then get on with her life, as far from the Maxwells as she could. Then, perhaps, Dominic's betrayal wouldn't be so—shatteringly painful.

But oh, he had been clever: letting her make all the running so that she came to him as sweetly as a tamed dove and almost begged him to make love to her. It had been a cruelly cunning move to let her initiate her own seduction, her own betrayal.

Their arrival back in New Zealand was hell. To begin with, there were journalists at Auckland airport, asking returning passengers their tales of the cyclone. Fenella turned her head away and refused to speak to any, but that was only the start.

The newspapers were full of items about the cyclone and its effect on Fala'isi; people were running concerts and conducting appeals for the homeless. Fenella donated as much as she could afford to one such appeal, then tried to put the whole thing out of her mind.

It proved to be impossible. As well as the newspaper headlines, almost every magazine Fenella picked up seemed to have an article on the cyclone, an article in

which Grant Chapman and Dominic featured widely.
Because they were so photogenic, she thought wildly.
They were lauded for the work they had done, the
dangers they had faced; one incident in particular, the
day she left Fala'isi, made her blood run cold. Dominic
had taken the helicopter to the edge of its range to rescue
some fishermen from a sinking vessel. There was talk
of a medal. It had been covered in the newspapers, but
the magazine journalist used her not inconsiderable
power with words to evoke the scene only too vividly.

Fenella's eyes scanned the article with a sick horror.
Overwritten and highly coloured though it was, there
was no way the journalist could magnify the danger.

In the photographs Dominic looked grim and reckless,
and there was a tall, pretty girl hanging on his arm who
was identified as Sarah Springfellow, his fiancée. The
journalist had clearly been fascinated to the point of ful-
someness with his handsome face and what she called
style and charisma. She had done some research too; she
gave details of Maxwell's search for the perfect cyclone-
proof dwelling, and a brief run-down on the company.

Fenella crumpled up the magazine as though it
poisoned her, then to her everlasting shame pulled out
the article and ironed it flat before hiding it in one of
her drawers.

Meantime Auckland's summer bloomed around them.
They spent Christmas with Anne and her family, and
Mark whiled away most of the holidays at the beach
polishing up his windsurfing skills and growing browner
and browner. Fenella ignored the heat and the humidity
and spent long hours in the flower shop and producing
pictures.

None of them mentioned Fala'isi or the Maxwells.

Fenella applied for a copy of her birth certificate, and
wasn't much surprised when it came back with the
father's name blank. What had really happened? Had
her mother been seduced and betrayed? Well, no one
would ever know now. But if that was so, it was no
wonder her mother had never had much time for her.

Her skin faded from its glowing tan to turn sallow, the exhaustion that had dogged her since their departure from Fala'isi increasing rather than going away, but it wasn't until she woke one morning feeling ill that her nascent suspicions burgeoned into fear.

That day she went into a chemist and bought a kit for pregnancy testing. She wasn't surprised at the positive results. But she was astounded at her own searing joy. Was this how her mother had felt when she conceived Mark, this excitement and delight, as though she had flung a challenge in the face of fortune, a challenge she had won?

Then common sense cast a pall over that first irrational delight. How on earth was she going to manage? What was she going to tell Mark? That another Maxwell bastard was on the way?

Fenella's soft red mouth twisted. The tears came softly, inexorably. She wept for the love that she would never know, for opportunities lost, for love offered and rejected. And she wept because her child would never know its father.

But she was determined on that point at least. The Maxwells had brought her family nothing but grief and pain, and she was not going to subject the child she carried to any of their particular form of family feeling.

The next day Anne sat her down with a cup of peppermint tea and commanded briskly, 'Tell me.'

Fenella looked at the wisps of steam rising from the pale surface of the liquid. 'I think you know,' she said quietly.

'I know you're not well.'

'Oh, I'm as well as can be expected. All things considered.'

Anne's breath hissed out. 'So you are pregnant!'

'Yes. I haven't seen a doctor yet, but yesterday I did one of those tests, and it was positive.'

Anne eyed her cautiously. 'Any chance of marrying the man?'

'No.' Only one syllable, but there was a wealth of disillusionment in it, enough to warn Anne off the subject.

'So what are you going to do?' At Fenella's puzzled glance she elaborated, 'You don't have to become a solo mother, you know. There are alternatives. Abortion or adoption...'

For Fenella was shaking her head. 'No. I'm not against either, but this baby I want.' She gave a sad little smile. 'It will probably be the only one I ever have.'

'Oh, come on now, don't give up so easily. OK, you've had a setback, but the world's full of decent men, and you're far from unattractive. You'll get married one day. And when you do there'll be other children. You like kids, and they like you, so you'll make a good mother.' Anne's bracing tone was like a tonic.

'I certainly intend to give it my best effort.'

Anne drank some of her coffee and mused, 'At least you'll be able to keep on working. We can rig up the playpen I used to have when my kids were little, and you'll be able to keep the baby with you when you paint.' She made a comical face. 'I feel for you, I really do, but I must confess I'm looking forward to it. It's time we had another baby around the place. I already think of myself as a cross between a grandmother and an aunt!'

Cheered by her friend's practical good sense, Fenella smiled widely. 'Aunt Anne has a nice ring to it,' she agreed.

From then on things were not quite so bad. She went to the doctor, who gave a prescription for vitamin pills with a stern injunction to take them because she was too pale. But it was not a lack of food that kept her pale, it was the pain eating away at her heart, the long hours she spent longing for a man who had discarded her in the most cruel way.

And no matter how much she tried to replace her grief with anger and contempt, as soon as she let her guard down the wearying emotions surged to the surface, draining her of energy and purpose and all her joy in life.

She thought she managed to put a good face on it until Mark, home for Easter, asked, 'What's the matter, Fen? Are you sick?'

'A little,' she said, covering up. 'Don't worry, I'll get over it.'

'It's because you're working so hard,' he said, frowning. 'You don't have to, you know. I'm going to get a job over the May holidays. Anne says I can be her delivery boy.'

One of the things that kept the business's overheads down was the converted butcher's cycle and the slightly retarded eighteen-year-old who used it to deliver flowers to nearby addresses.

'Really? She didn't tell me you were taking over for Joey.'

'He's going to stay with his grandmother in Brisbane.'

'I see. Well, I'm sure you'll be an excellent delivery boy,' Fenella said. 'Make sure you're careful and—hey, wait a minute, you usually go away in May.'

Mark shrugged, looking a little uneasy. 'Oh, I told the Head I wasn't going anywhere this year.'

Treading delicately, Fenella said, 'I think you should love, if they want you to.'

'No. I'm going to work; plenty of the guys get holiday jobs, you know, and I'm old enough to earn my share.'

He said no more, leaving the subject of Fenella's overwork, to her great relief. Sooner or later he would have to learn that she was pregnant, but not just yet. And she certainly wasn't going to tell him that she was saving up as much as she could now in case she couldn't put in as much work after the baby's birth. Her hand stole to her stomach. Already the skin there was tighter, the slight thickening of her slenderness as yet the only indication of the child who lay so securely under her heart. It wouldn't be long before her condition became obvious, but until then she would keep silence.

Mark went back to school and she resumed the frenetic pace of her life, organising whole dinner parties and 'occasions' as the autumn social scene began to heat up.

One dark evening she arrived home cold and wet, because the day had started out fine and she had neglected to take an umbrella. Her lips were blue and chattering, and she was in a temper; the hostess whose flowers she had been organising kept changing her mind and at the last minute decided on several changes that meant a lot of fiddling about.

Wearily Fenella discarded her clothes and sank into a bath, soaking the cold and the tiredness away, lying with her neck supported on a rolled-up towel until the tight muscles eased in relaxation.

She had dried herself down and was smoothing almond oil into the stretching skin of her waistline when the doorbell rang.

'Go away,' she muttered, looking out at the rain slashing down on to the window.

But the bell rang again, imperative, commanding.

Hauling on her old ice-pink dressing-gown, she went out through the small sitting-room and across to the door. It was on the chain, so she opened it.

'I'm glad to see you have some regard for your safety,' said Dominic, his glittering eyes raking her from her scrubbed face to the bare toes that peeped out from under the hem of her dressing-gown. 'Let me in.'

CHAPTER NINE

AFTERWARDS Fenella decided that his sudden appearance must have bewitched her, for she unhooked the chain without demur, stepping back to allow him in.

He loomed over her in the small hallway, rain-slicked hair darkened from charcoal-brown to black, well-cut overcoat sodden across the wide shoulders. When he shrugged out of it she saw that he wore a superbly tailored pin-striped suit. It should have looked ridiculously formal. That it didn't was a tribute to the overwhelming magnetism of the man.

Slinging the coat on to the bentwood coat stand, he turned to look at her, his expression grim. 'What the hell have you been doing to yourself?' he demanded.

'Nothing.' Her voice sounded remote. For an ecstatic moment she thought he had come for her, but one glimpse of the antagonism in his expression and she knew she had been indulging in wishful thinking.

Thank heavens she was dressed in the nearest approximation to a tent she had in her wardrobe! Not even his keen eyes would be able to see beneath its voluminous pink folds to gather any evidence of her pregnancy.

'Don't be a fool,' he said roughly. 'You've been pushing yourself too hard. His housemaster tells me that even Mark is worried about you, and I don't need to tell you that this is an important year for him at school.'

'No,' she said dully, turning away, 'no, you don't need to tell me.' Of course it was Mark he had come to see.

'So why the shadows under your eyes?' He sounded angry, and when she gave no answer, merely lifting her shoulders in a shrug, that anger was transmuted into action.

Catching her chin, he lifted it, bringing up his other hand to touch the fine skin under her eyes with a gentle forefinger. 'What is it, Fenella?' he asked, his voice softening into a murmur. 'What's the matter?'

Mesmerised, her eyes so deep a blue they were almost black, she searched his face, noting that he too had driven himself hard and fast in the four and a half months since she had seen him last. He looked leaner, the brutal beauty of his features honed to a sharper, more cutting edge. But there was amusement flickering in the dense green depths of his gaze, and a smoky hunger that chilled her heart.

'How's Sarah Springfellow?' she asked politely. 'The woman you're engaged to?'

His fingers tightened unbearably on her chin, then relaxed, letting her pull free.

'I am not engaged to her,' he said with a calm certainty that convinced her he was speaking the truth. 'I've never been engaged to her, and I have no intention of becoming engaged to her in the future. She's eighteen—slightly too young for me, wouldn't you think?'

'I suppose it depends on what you want in a wife,' she returned woodenly, striving to repress yet another useless pulse of hope in her heart. His mother had lied—perhaps she had lied about everything!

But no, she had known they had been lovers. And he had to have told her that. And he had organised Sarah Springfellow's passage up to Fala'isi in the Learjet . . .

Hope died, collapsed into blackened ashes. Fenella said remotely, 'What do you want, Dominic?'

He seemed to have changed tack. The open aggression was gone, replaced by a hard confidence that alarmed her more than his antagonism. His eyes were like polished jade, depthless, coolly assessing as they surveyed her.

'I confess I liked you better in the bathrobe you wore when you came to me in Fala'isi,' he said cruelly, watching with cynical amusement as her colour faded, then came scalding back. 'You were the perfect lover, the ideal mistress. There's nothing like satin against satin skin to appeal to a man. The one you're wearing now looks—domestic. But then you weren't expecting to seduce anyone tonight, were you? I must say, Fenella, you learned well from your first lover.'

'Will you go, please?'

'No. Now that I'm here, I might as well find out what made you run from me on Fala'isi. I thought I'd pleasured you well enough; if I didn't come up to scratch I'd be delighted to try again.' He smiled with calculating savagery as she flinched away. 'I know a few more—esoteric—tricks that might interest you.'

Fenella thought she heard the sound of her heart breaking, felt it shatter into shards. Through lips stiff with pain and anger she said, 'I think you've said quite enough, Dominic. Please go.'

'I'm damned if I will! I want to know why you lay in my arms all night through, and then ran like hell the next day as though your only chance of survival was to put as much distance as you could between us. Why, damn you?'

The words were snarled out with such menace that for a moment their meaning failed to register. When it did, the feral coldness of his fury ignited Fenella's.

'Don't try to intimidate me,' she said heatedly, prudently removing herself to behind the nearest chair. 'I left because you told me to.'

'When? When I woke you up to tell you that I had to go, that there was a fishing boat calling for help?' The beautifully sculpted lips were marred by a sneer. 'When I left you sleeping so sweetly in my bed, your long golden limbs gleaming with love and satiation? Did you think that if you left me I'd come running after you, so hot for you that I'd pay your price to get you back into my bed?'

'No!' The hands she clapped to her ears were hauled ruthlessly down.

'What was the price?' he asked, dragging them across so that they rested on his chest, just above his heart.

'Did you want marriage, Fenella? Too bad, because I don't want to marry someone like you. An affair—well, that's different. I'm more than happy to have an affair with you, but it will be on my terms.'

Her fingers spread, reacting to the heavy pace of his heart beneath. She said hopelessly, 'I won't have an affair with you.'

'Oh, I think you would. Depending, perhaps, on how well I sweeten the pot.' He smiled into her horrified face with calculated charm. 'You should have waited, Fenella, so that we could discuss terms. Of course I'll look after you, until I tire of you.'

Each word struck her like a blow, driving the colour from her face. She swayed, and he grabbed her, lifting her high in his arms. 'What the hell is the matter with you?' he demanded.

Desperately she managed to struggle free, holding herself stiffly away so that she didn't come into contact with the lean length of him.

'Please go, Dominic, I can't take much more of this.'

'Then tell me why you left Fala'isi.' He was remorseless, his uncompromising authority never so obvious as now, when he was determined to get the truth.

Looking away from the hard determination of his arrogant face, Fenella subsided on to the sofa and said quietly, 'I left because—because your mother told me you had asked her to get rid of me.'

He was like stone, obdurate, unforgiving, disbelieving. 'Don't lie, Fenella. You were gone before my mother arrived. And even if this farrago were true, you know I wouldn't have asked her to get rid of you.'

'Why?'

'Because when I woke you to tell you why I was leaving you, I told you how much I'd enjoyed what we did together. I told you!' he snarled.

Not giving an inch, her face as cold and smooth and unrevealing as a statue, she said quietly, 'What time did you wake me?'

'At four-thirty——' He stopped, brought his fury under control, then began again in the level hard tone she hated. 'The call came in from Grant Chapman just before dawn and I woke you and told you I had to go, but you were to wait for me, I'd be back.' His gaze ran insolently, lustfully, down the length of her body. 'I also told you that you were all I'd ever dreamed of, warm and passionate and uninhibited, and that I was going to find it bloody hard to concentrate because all I wanted to do was lose myself in the manifold erotic delights of that compliant body.'

Colour scorching up through her sallow skin, Fenella protested indignantly, 'You said no such thing!'

'I did. And you know it, you lying little cheat, because you answered, you asked me when I'd be back, why I had to go. But when I got back you'd run away like the coward you are. I concluded that your first experience with me hadn't lived up to expectations or that you wanted more than I was prepared to offer.'

Her heart breaking, she said tonelessly, 'When I woke up in the morning you'd gone, and within an hour your mother had arrived.'

Dominic bared his teeth. 'Don't try——'

Anguish roughened her voice as she cried, 'She gave me your instructions—get the hell off the island!'

Flatly, dangerously, he said, 'I know she arrived the day you left.' He paused, then resumed coldly, 'When I got home she was waiting for me, but she hadn't seen you—you and Mark had left before she got there.'

Anger and a strong sense of injustice strengthened her voice. 'I suppose you're in the habit of believing her, but I know she was there, Dominic. She wore a pair of linen trousers, pale beige, with a top the same colour and a wide mauve belt. Over it she had a mauve jacket, and she wore a solitaire diamond on the third finger of her right hand.' Even when she closed her eyes she could see Louise Maxwell's image. It was burned on to her brain.

His brows drew together; after a moment he said in an arrested voice, 'Yes, she wears her mother's ring on that hand.'

Fenella was silent. He had to make up his own mind; the choice was his. If he believed his mother then there was no prospect of any sort of future for them.

His frown deepened. In an edged tone he demanded, 'But why would she lie to me?'

It was Fenella's turn to shrug. 'I don't know.' Something compelled her to add, 'Mark and I went back to the airport in the same taxi she and Sarah Springfellow arrived in. If you really wanted to check that out, I imagine you could.'

His dark gleaming head whipped around to spear her with a savage glare. 'Sarah didn't come until three days later.'

Fenella went white. 'What? But she said——' And she stopped, realising how easily Louise Maxwell had tricked her.

He scanned her remote pale face, his own set in lines as hard and clear-cut as a mask. Only his eyes moved, shimmering with an unknown emotion as they searched her face. In a toneless voice he pressed, 'Why did you leave Maxwell's Reach? What did my mother say?'

'I told you.'

'Tell me again, Fenella.'

The words came with almost no emphasis, but after a fleeting glance at his harsh features she ran her tongue over suddenly dry lips and capitulated. She knew now why he was so respected and feared amongst his peers.

'That you'd asked her to—get rid of me.' Not to him, not to anyone, would she reveal the sordid name-calling of that interview, the older woman's malice and contempt. However she had behaved to Mark and Fenella, Louise Maxwell must love her son. And presumably he loved her. 'That I was in the way. That you were engaged to Sarah Springfellow.'

'And you believed her?'

'I had no reason not to. You'd made no attempt to hide what you thought of me. And your name has been linked to hers.'

'After the night we spent together, you thought I could use my mother to do such dirty work?'

His incredulity hurt. With bleak bitterness she retorted, 'Men sleep with women they despise often enough to make it not exactly unusual behaviour. As your mother pointed out.'

Deep in the wintry eyes, bleak as ice on a mountain top, a flame flickered, hidden yet fierce.

Defensively she said, 'And in spite of what you say, you didn't tell me anything that morning. But I wouldn't have gone if your mother hadn't—damn it, I heard you talking about the Learjet the night before! You said they were coming on it. You knew they were coming and you left me to—to——' She stopped, biting her lips to keep them from trembling, but she wasn't able to keep the terrible impact of his betrayal from her voice.

'I knew the Learjet was coming,' he said harshly. 'I ordered the Sydney operation to gather up as much in the way of foodstuffs as they could and get it the hell up there. But I didn't know my mother would arrive up on it. I was furious with her—she took up room that was needed for far more important things! What exactly did you overhear me say?'

She thought, summoning the memory from the depths of her brain where she had pushed it. 'That somebody was coming up on the Learjet the next day,' she said slowly, a cautious hope struggling to grow in the wastelands of her heart.

'Not someone—something.'

She nodded. Of course it could have been that; she had heard no name, but persuaded by Louise Maxwell's lies had jumped to conclusions.

Miserably, she said, 'But she knew we'd—that we were——'

'Were lovers?' he supplied, his mouth hardening. 'By looking at you, I suppose. It was easy enough to see.'

And then he snapped, 'Of course! Why the hell didn't I remember?'

Bewildered, she demanded, 'What? Remember what?'

'That first day you were on Fala'isi Mark told us that he'd often conducted quite reasonable conversations with you when you were asleep. Remember, he was teasing you about it, and you were uncomfortable, I could tell you hated him talking about it. Too intimate, I suppose. I'd forgotten completely about it, but that must have been what happened. I thought you'd woken, it never occurred to me that you were still asleep.' He stared down at her accusingly. 'Damn it, Fenella, you sounded as though you were awake!'

Shaken, her eyes wide with disbelief, she said in a stunned voice, 'Do you mean that if you'd known—if I'd woken—no, I don't believe it!'

But she did, and with her belief came the realisation that it would have solved nothing; she had left because she believed his mother's lies.

And he had never said a word of love; he wanted her, but he thought in terms of an affair. She shook her head, saying miserably, 'It means nothing. It wouldn't work, it was a mistake, we should never have made love. You resent me.'

'Yes,' he said simply. When she would have turned away he grabbed her wrist and held her, without hurting her but with his lean fingers laced so that she couldn't get away. 'Oh, yes, I resent it, because it's so bloody obvious you don't feel the same way. I despised my father for falling for your mother, even though I understood why; she was beautiful, with a kind of careless sensuality that promised far too much to a man starved of love and laughter. You've met my mother; you can imagine he got damned little of either from her, poor devil. But I thought your mother had sucked him in, that she wanted an easy life. Even when she killed herself, I wouldn't admit that it was because she loved him. I told myself—and you—that it was because she had no claim on us, that she'd have to work. Then I kissed you, and

I damned near went up in flames. You were only sixteen, still a child, and I wanted nothing more than to take you to bed and bury myself in the innocent witchery of your body until I'd made it impossible for you to ever look at another man.'

He smiled, a mirthless stretching of his lips, his leaping eyes slowly scanning the pale shame in her expression. 'I was young and arrogant and cruel,' he said austerely. 'Cruel to you because I despised myself for being as weak as my father, able to see beneath the surface trickery of form and colouring and texture to the conniving woman beneath, yet still wanting you, just as he'd wanted your mother.'

His hand contracted and she gasped. Swearing beneath his breath, he loosened his grip, staring down at the contrast of swarthy fingers against the pale fragility of her wrist. 'I'd just been through my father's accounts,' he said angrily, 'and been appalled by how much your mother had bled him. Your school fees, the house, her own extensive and elaborate wardrobe, jewellery—which she swore she didn't own—everything had come from his pocket. I thought she was a greedy opportunist.'

Her lashes fell. 'And you thought I was like her.'

'It was safer for me to think that! Just as it was safer for me to refuse to admit that she could have cost him a packet, yet still love him. But after kissing you—hell, I was running scared. And I'd always championed my mother.' His mouth twisted in a chilling little smile. 'You could say I was reared to do that. Oh, I'd known for some years that her invalidism was more a matter of mind than reality, but she'd had a pretty thin time of it with my father. And he, poor devil, with her. They should never have married.'

Something in his voice caught Fenella's attention. She thought of a small boy caught in a kind of tug-of-war between his parents, and her heart melted. Without thinking she brought her free hand up and covered his.

'Feeling sorry for me?' He didn't miss anything. The smile became even more twisted. 'If that's all you can feel, I'll take it. I never thought I'd say this, but I'll take anything I can get from you.'

She said sadly, 'Even though all you want is to make love to me?'

'That's not all that I want. I find in myself a capacity for possessiveness that appals me. I want you, mind, body and soul. I want to know that when you think of me you smile, that you ache for me, miss me when I'm not here, that you need me as much as I need you.'

'I won't——' But she was wavering, and he knew it. Unable to continue, she bit her lip.

He smiled, his expression filled with the indomitable will she dreaded. 'Yes, you will,' he said confidently.

Her chin lifted. 'No.'

Something moved in the pale depths of his eyes. She thought of sharks in the lagoon, and shivered. 'Do you want to punish me a little?' he asked pleasantly. 'Fair enough, but I can think of better ways to make me suffer than this. Ways that you'll enjoy just as much as I will.'

Her heart leapt, then sank. She said quietly, 'No.'

'Why?'

She turned her head away and the quick, useless tears magnified her eyes. Blinking ferociously, she tried to banish them, but Dominic must have seen, because he pulled her up off the sofa and into his arms, holding her gently but firmly against him.

She saw the moment when he realised, the moment the arrogant self-confidence in his face was replaced by shock, rapidly followed by black fury. His lashes came down, hiding his thoughts, but Fenella shivered at what she saw there, and waited like a doe at bay for the blow to fall.

His hand slid from her breast down to her waist, lingering, probing.

After a moment he said in the silken savage voice of ultimate rage, 'I see.'

She bit her lip, ready to tell him that if he was interested in the child she would not deny him access, but he forestalled her. In a voice so remote that it froze her blood he said, 'I suppose I should be thankful that at least you have the decency not to palm off another man's child on to me.'

He was gone before Fenella could let her astonishment compel her to blurt out the truth, and by the time she realised that he had gone, her anger had exploded in a red haze. She stood for long moments staring down at her clenched fists, then flung a cushion on to the ground with a violent oath, wishing she could hit him hard on that beautiful, smug, brutal face, rearrange his features so that no other woman would ever fall into their specious snare.

Even as she thought it she knew she was wrong. She had not fallen in love with his looks, not even with his personal magnetism. She had fallen in love with the man, and it didn't seem to matter that he had just insulted her again; she was grimly aware that in some way she was probably going to love him until she died.

The next morning she wasn't able to get out of bed. Reaction, she thought miserably as she lay aching and heartsick, wondering if she was ever going to be able to keep her breakfast down again. The cream crackers she had beside her bed didn't help at all.

Groaning, she rang Anne to tell her she'd be late for work.

'No problem,' Anne assured her. 'But shouldn't you have stopped this by now? I seem to remember that I felt fine after the third month.'

'I've been quite good for a few weeks. This must just be an isolated incident.'

'OK, love. Don't push yourself. Spend the day in bed. We're not going to be busy, there's too much rain about. I'll hop around after school when the kids come home and see how you are.'

The telephone rang a couple of times. Fenella had forgotten to switch on the answerphone, but after the first time, when she had had to veer off to the bathroom, she ignored it. In a daze of misery and fear, half convinced that she was losing her baby, she lay still and stiff in the bed, obsessively going over every moment of the confrontation from the night before, hoarding every fleeting nuance of his voice, the moments when he had said he wanted her, the blaze of emotion she had seen in his eyes warming the pale green to emerald.

It was the middle of the afternoon before she felt well enough to crawl out of bed, and even then she couldn't bring herself to eat anything more than dry toast. With it she drank peppermint tea, lying back on the sofa, her pale face filled with foreboding, trying to summon up the energy to ring her doctor for an appointment. She had managed to get as far as leaving the chain off the door so that Anne, who had her own key, could come in, but the thought of doing anything else made her stomach lurch in a very sinister way.

But it was not Anne who unlocked the door. It was the caretaker, and with him was Dominic, his handsome gladiator's face dark with some suppressed emotion.

'I'm sorry,' the caretaker said, looking put out, 'but you weren't answering your phone and this gentleman seemed to think there might be something wrong——'

'I've been sick,' Fenella said, smiling palely at the middle-aged man, carefully avoiding Dominic's eyes. 'Thank you for worrying.'

'Well, that's all right.' From the resentful glance he directed upwards it seemed only too clear that Dominic had been his usual autocratic self. 'You want to be careful, it's the change of season—everyone gets the flu, it seems.'

Grumbling slightly, he removed himself, leaving Dominic very much inside.

Fenella stared at the floor, saying tiredly, 'I can't cope with this, Dominic.'

'I can see that.' His voice had ice crystals in it. 'Why isn't your lover looking after you?'

'He's no longer in the picture,' she said, exhaustion dragging her voice down.

'What happened?' He didn't wait for an answer, just went into her bedroom. From his movements she fancied he was stripping the bed. Surely, she thought, light-headed by now, he didn't expect to find her lover between the sheets?

'Get out of there.' Was that her voice, trembling with emotion, weak and wretched?

Emerging, he came across to where she sat and swung her up in his arms.

'Put me down!'

'Shut up,' he said grimly, and carried her into her bedroom. He had made the narrow tumbled bed and pulled the blankets back. He stood her on her feet, removed the pink dressing-gown he had been so scathing about, and without saying a word propelled her back into bed. She surged up, but had to settle back with a moan as the rapid movement made her stomach lurch ominously.

'Who's your doctor?' he demanded.

'She can't come——'

'Of course she can come. That's what she's there for.'

She did too, and told them that the baby was fine, but that Fenella was to avoid any emotional upsets. Thoroughly charmed by Dominic, she had responded with true feminine appreciation to his dangerous charisma, telling him that Fenella needed looking after and that she was working too hard.

When he came back Fenella flared weakly, 'I don't want you here, Dominic.'

'I know you don't but as you're too ill to get up and there doesn't seem to be anyone else who can look after you, you'll have to put up with me.'

He refused to go, refused to fight with her, made her more tea and toast and forced her to eat it, carried her into the bathroom and stood by while she washed her face and cleaned her teeth, told Anne when she rang that it didn't matter that she was unable to come, he was looking after Fenella, and generally took over, ignoring Fenella's efforts to get rid of him.

He was still there when she drifted off to sleep, unaccountably feeling cherished and protected as she never had before, and when she woke in the morning, miraculously recovered, she found him sprawled out asleep on the sofa bed in the sitting-room, clad, so far as she could see, in nothing.

Her heart lurched. He woke instantly, and said in his sleep-roughened voice, 'How are you this morning?'

'I'm fine.' She eyed the splendid male torso with helpless fascination. He stretched, muscles popping and rippling, then began to fling back the blankets. Fenella disappeared.

The delectable smell of coffee had permeated the kitchen by the time Dominic came out of the bathroom clad in his casual shirt and trousers. As she took two pieces of toast from the toaster Fenella said in her curtest tone, 'You must have had an uncomfortable night.'

'Not anywhere near as uncomfortable as the one before,' he said cryptically.

'I'm sorry I've only got toast to eat.'

He looked quizzical, the deadly anger she had aroused apparently entirely gone. 'It'll do. Tell me, what did you mean when you said the baby's father was no longer in the offing?'

She poured boiling water over a teaspoon of Earl Grey tea and put the lid on the teapot. 'Just that,' she said, her voice even and arid.

'No possibility of getting together again?'

'No. Not,' she added belatedly, 'that's it's any of your business.'

'Well, in that case, you'd better marry me.'

She stared at his closed expression, her eyes huge in her pale face, while she tried to take in the enormity of this. 'Who told you?' she stammered. 'How did you find out? No one knew, I didn't tell anyone...'

His eyes narrowed, sharpened into pinpoints of green crystal. 'Who told me what?'

'That the baby——' She stopped, clamping her mouth tight.

His smile was tigerish. 'It occurred to me an hour or so after I'd left you,' he said pleasantly, buttering a piece of toast, 'and you've just confirmed it.'

She shook her head, avoiding the pale glitter of his gaze. 'Well, it doesn't matter,' she said. 'I'm not going to marry you.'

'Why?'

With her back presented adamantly to him, she leaned against the bench, hands clenched on the edge. 'Because you would never know why I married you,' she said at last, staring blindly out of the window. 'And I know what you think of women who trap men with pregnancy. You've made your opinion of that sort of behaviour very clear.'

'And if I told you that I've rarely regretted anything as much as I do the things I said about your mother?'

She shrugged. 'You wouldn't have said them if you didn't believe them. People very rarely change their most deep-seated beliefs.' She risked a look at him, saw that he was still watching her from beneath lowered lashes, his gaze very keen and alert. 'I couldn't live with that.'

'And if I told you that I loved you? That I've loved you since I first saw you, and that all my rantings and ravings were merely my futile efforts to persuade myself otherwise?'

Oh, but she wanted to believe him. She wanted so much to believe him that she could taste it, but she knew better. With a wise, sad little smile she said, 'I wouldn't believe you.'

'In that case,' he said quietly, 'I'll have to try other tactics, won't I?'

Fenella swung around, her attention held by something unusual in the deep tones. He was smiling, although there was no humour in his expression, merely a driving determination that made her shrink back.

'Come and sit down,' he said calmly, waiting until she had done so before saying, 'As you seem to think that all I want is the child, I could wait until it's born and then apply for custody. Or, as apparently you're convinced that I'm convinced you only got pregnant for mercenary reasons, I could suggest a mercenary marriage, with iron-clad contracts signed by both parties. Or I could woo you until you give in to the fact that you want me just as much as I want you——'

'Stop it!' she whispered, her hands coming up to cover her face.

He came around the table and picked her up, carrying her effortlessly into the bedroom. There he sat on the side of the bed and held her against him, saying nothing until her trembling had stopped. He was very strong; she rested her head against him and listened to the thud of his heart, smelt the indefinable, infinitely reassuring scent of warm male.

'How many men have you slept with?' he asked. 'Besides your first lover.'

Very quietly, she said, 'I didn't sleep with Paul.'

She expected disbelief, but he probed, 'And there's been no one else either, has there?'

'No.'

He laughed, a self-derisory little sound. 'I was as sure as I could be of anything that that was so. You were so—so innocent. So surprised by what I did to you, so rapturously, joyously amazed at your own reactions. All that day as I flew people around in the chopper, I kept thinking of how you'd been, so fiery that my body tightened just thinking about it, yet sweet and loving—and always, that surprise, as though you'd never known a man before. I told myself that it was because you'd only slept with a man twenty years older than you that you'd responded like that, but I knew in my heart that you'd been a virgin. And when I accepted that, I accepted that whatever had happened when I kissed you first had happened to both of us. I came home, prepared to suggest marriage, convinced that you'd jump at it, and you were gone.'

Fenella said, 'I left because your mother said you were engaged to Sarah Springfellow. I was sure she was right because when I went in to you that night, you were dreaming about her. You said her name.'

'Did I?' He sounded shaken. 'Possibly because I've been doing my best to avoid her for the past year. Her mother and mine think marriage would be a good idea.'

Recalling Louise Maxwell's brutal summing up of Sarah's advantages and Fenella's lack of them, she said in a troubled voice, 'Perhaps they're right.'

'Was my mother unpleasant?'

She shivered at the steely note in his voice. 'Yes, but it wasn't that. I can deal with that,' she said. 'I'm not afraid of her.'

'Mark?'

She hesitated, then said fairly, 'You can't expect her to like him.'

'Possibly not, but when we're married she'll behave.'

At last she lifted her head, staring into his face, her own anguished. 'Dominic, I don't know...'

'Yes, you do,' he said, his calm voice belied by the pulse that beat rapidly in his jaw. 'You love me, and I love you. We've been in love for the past seven years, we just didn't realise it. We're going to stay in love for the rest of our lives, so we might as well get married and make Mark and Grandfather pleased, as well as giving our child a settled, idyllically happy home.'

Her mouth quivered. 'I'm so tempted,' she said at last, 'but——'

'Give in to temptation for once.'

A lurking smile touched her lips, then fled. 'But your mother——'

'My mother,' Dominic said calmly and without any sign of affection, 'will do as she's told. She's an embittered, malicious woman, but she can't hurt you or Mark because neither Grandfather nor I take any notice of her malice or her self-pity. You won't have to worry about her, I promise you. And Grandfather likes you, which means much more to me than my mother's feelings.'

Fenella hadn't his hard-eyed pragmatism, or his cynical view of Louise, but she gave in, promising herself that he would learn that mothers could love their children as she suspected he had not been loved. Still, she had to say, 'I don't think I'm the sort of person you should marry, Dominic. I'm not social——'

'Neither am I,' he interrupted swiftly, sliding his hands along her arms to enclose her cold hands in his big warm ones. 'I hate socialising, unless it's with friends. So if you want to spend your nights at charity balls or gallery openings, you'll have to go without me most of the time. I love you, and to me that means being with you as much as I possibly can. I can organise my workload so that I don't have to travel nearly as much as I do now. And after the children come, we'll both be there for them.'

Fenella surrendered, persuaded as much by the warmth and tenderness in his eyes as by the softened note in his voice when he talked of their life together. He had never lied to her, not even when it would be easy to, not when it might have been kinder to. He was a man who could be trusted, a man who told the truth as he saw it. He said he loved her; slowly, tremulously, she was allowing herself to believe that he did.

'No prep school when they're seven?' She smiled enticingly up at him.

'No,' he said, his lips a fraction of an inch away from hers. 'Not that it did either of us any harm, did it?'

She chuckled. He would be no soft touch, this man she loved, even with that lovelight gleaming deep in his eyes.

And then he kissed her, and she forgot about her reservations, forgot about anything but the tide of passion that leaped up to meet him.

'I want you so much,' he said against her mouth.

'I want you too.'

'But you were so ill yesterday.'

She kissed him, touching his bottom lip with her tongue, rejoicing at the sudden deep breath he took. 'I think it was reaction. I feel fine now—truly.'

But still he held back, so she took the dominant part, seducing him with a shy wantonness until he could no longer resist her.

Afterwards, when they were lying entwined, she said on a caught breath, 'I think—oh, Dominic, I think our baby moved!' She grabbed his hand, but the tiny flutter died away. Nevertheless, his hand remained on her abdomen, resting there with possessive pride.

'I can't wait,' he said, kissing her, the drawn contours of passion replaced by satisfaction and tenderness.

The last faint wisps of doubt faded. He couldn't speak like that, look at her with such love and passion, if he thought she had used her body and the baby to get him to marry her.

'Shadows in those midnight eyes? What is it?' he asked perceptively.

Fenella told him, and he kissed the slight thickening about her waist, his mouth wonderfully gentle. 'I was wrong. You knew I was wrong, and, deep down, I did too. I fell in love with you, didn't I? I wouldn't fall in love with a woman who used her body as a trading stamp.'

'As my mother did,' she said sadly.

He shrugged, sliding up the narrow bed to pull her close into his arms and hold her. 'I don't know. I'm not the intense judgemental kid that I was when I first found out about her. I think she must have loved Dad and wanted to tie him to her in the only way she could think of. Otherwise, why did his betrayal, because that's really what it was, wasn't it, bring her to such misery that she killed herself? Neither of them were exactly courageous, were they? Perhaps we should just let them rest in peace now. They may be together again, who knows? He certainly died with her name on his lips.'

'Thank you,' Fenella said softly.

'The past is theirs,' he said. 'The future is ours, with all its promise and joy. The storm is over, my heart.'

In a gesture of complete trust Fenella turned her face into his throat, feeling the strong life force beat through his pulse. Yes, the storm was gone, and the future stretched fair and serene in front of them.

HARLEQUIN PRESENTS®

A Year Down Under

Beginning in January 1993, some of Harlequin Presents's most exciting authors will join us as we celebrate the land down under by featuring one title per month set in Australia or New Zealand.

Intense, passionate romances, these stories will take you from the heart of the Australian outback to the wilds of New Zealand, from the sprawling cattle and sheep stations to the sophistication of cities like Sydney and Auckland.

Share the adventure—and the romance— of A Year Down Under!

Don't miss our first visit in HEART OF THE OUTBACK by Emma Darcy, Harlequin Presents #1519, available in January wherever Harlequin Books are sold.   YDU-G

HARLEQUIN  PRESENTS®

is

- ☑ exotic
- ☑ dramatic
- ☑ sensual
- ☑ exciting
- ☑ contemporary
- ☑ a fast, involving read
- ☑ terrific!!

Harlequin Presents—
passionate romances
around the world!

HARLEQUIN ROMANCE®

After her father's heart attack, Stephanie Bloomfield comes home to Orchard Valley, Oregon, to be with him and with her sisters.

Orchard Valley

Steffie learns that many things have changed in her absence—but not her feelings for journalist Charles Tomaselli. He was the reason she left Orchard Valley. Now, three years later, will he give her a reason to stay?

"The Orchard Valley trilogy features three delightful, spirited sisters and a trio of equally fascinating men. The stories are rich with the romance, warmth of heart and humor readers expect, and invariably receive, from Debbie Macomber."

—Linda Lael Miller

Don't miss the Orchard Valley trilogy by Debbie Macomber:

VALERIE   Harlequin Romance #3232 (November 1992)
STEPHANIE   Harlequin Romance #3239 (December 1992)
NORAH   Harlequin Romance #3244 (January 1993)

Look for the special cover flash on each book!

Available wherever Harlequin books are sold.   ORC-2

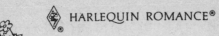